CW01596973

SAVKAR ALTINEL was born in Istanbul. After completing secondary education there, he left Türkiye and studied English literature at the University of Chicago and the University of Glasgow. He then carved out a literary career for himself by continuing to live in Britain while writing in Turkish. A combination that could easily have turned him into the traditional victim "caught between two cultures" becomes, in his case, a source of strength that enables him to view everything with the cold, dispassionate gaze of a passing stranger. Widely recognised in his country of birth as a poet and a translator of English poetry whose range includes work by Donne, Coleridge, Kipling, Ted Hughes and Philip Larkin, he is also known for a number of genre-bending prose works deftly blending travel writing and auto-fiction. Sometimes compared to W. G. Sebald in this respect, but very much with preoccupations and a voice of his own, he is one of the most interesting and significant figures in contemporary Turkish literature.

THOUSAND HORSEMEN PRESS

4A Brassie Avenue W3 7DE London
www.thousandhorsemenpress.com
info@thousandhorsemenpress.com

Copyright © Savkar Altinel, 2004
Translation © Savkar Altinel, 2024
Originally published in the Turkish by YKY
with the title *Kvangvamun Kavşağı*

All rights reserved. This book or any portion thereof may not be reproduced or used in any manner whatsoever without the express written permission of Thousand Horsemen Press, except for the use of brief quotations in a book review.

978-1-0682097-1-0

First edition by Thousand Horsemen Press in 2026

Translated from the Turkish by Savkar Altinel

Edited by Fionn Petch

Typeset by M. Hakan Güngör

Printed and bound by Pureprint (UK)

2 4 6 8 9 7 5 3 1

WILD ROADS

SAVKAR ALTINEL

In memory of H.
who was fond of travel and words
and C.
who didn't venture outdoors in the last decade of her life.

Let's fly to the famous Asian cities,
Stealing our maps from dark museums.

—Henri Coulette

AT THE FIELD MARSHAL'S HOME

In Helsinki the sea was frozen. The light snow, falling since my arrival in the city nearly an hour earlier, had done the rest, rendering the handful of vessels moored in the harbour invisible by draping itself over them like camouflage netting. If a small ferry hadn't been making its way through the ice with a curious hissing sound, I might not even have realised that the expanse of white with a rough surface resembling curdled milk that lay before me was not solid ground but part of the Gulf of Finland.

Having allowed myself to be brought here at short notice by a free weekend and a perpetual readiness to go somewhere at any excuse, I was dressed a little inadequately for the climate. All that supplemented the thick coat and trousers I normally wore at this time of the year was a fleece-lined hunter's cap which, bought during my time as an undergraduate in Chicago but never worn then or later, had somehow survived every move from house to house and country to country over the years, when so much else had simply vanished. With its earflaps pulled down and tied under my chin, I looked like the American I had never been and no longer had the option of becoming. I could have been taken for someone called Hank from Wisconsin.

I watched the ferry uncertainly as, its navigation lights burning in the late afternoon gloom, it moved towards an island amidst the ice some distance from the mouth of the harbour. Judging by a piece in the in-flight magazine I had flipped through on the plane, Helsinki was a city of strange museums (the Tram Museum, the Museum of Workers' Housing). Most of these had little appeal for me, but I couldn't spend all my time wandering the streets in a place where the temperature was twelve below zero and the pavements were under a layer of snow unlikely to disappear until the spring. Another museum, the home of Marshal Mannerheim who had repelled the attempted invasion of Finland by the Russians during the Second World War, and later served as the country's president, sounded like a more interesting choice. Apparently it was also conveniently located on a hill overlooking the harbour: I could walk there in five to ten minutes, spend some time indoors and get warm.

Quickly crossing the boulevard, half-empty because of the cold despite it being a Saturday, I began climbing up a side street I hoped would take me to my goal and, before long, found myself in a deserted road by a park resembling a winterscape by an Old Master with its leafless black trees standing against the dazzlingly white snow. Most of the colonnaded stone buildings and the pastel-coloured wooden Baltic houses with verandas and towers beyond the park were occupied by embassies. My lungs burning with the cold, I made my way past the French, Italian and Brazilian missions and walked on.

At the mouth of a street which ascended to the left opposite the pink-and-white Dutch Embassy, a metal sign half covered in snow indicated this was the way to the Mannerheim Museum. As I was approaching the sign, an Alsatian appeared in the grounds of the Estonian Embassy behind it and, barking loudly in the silence, wanted to know who I was. Yet the interrogation was a little half-hearted, as if he knew I had no real answer to give to such a question. Without bothering to reply, I pressed on, reached a white two-storey wooden house on top of the hill, and, wiping away the snowflakes that had settled on my face, went in.

Inside, a rather sullen-looking girl was seated at a table with a small revolving stand full of postcards of Mannerheim on it, and behind her, an old man and a blonde woman, who had their backs to me, were busy taking off their coats in front of a row of hooks on the wall. I was bending down towards the postcards to take a closer look at Mannerheim when the girl, alerted to the fact I was a foreigner unfamiliar with the Marshal, intervened, saying, "If you want to visit the Museum, you'll need to hurry; this'll be the last English-language tour today."

For a second I looked at her, feeling a little disconcerted. Discovering that I had to join a guided tour to see the museum was not welcome news. As I preferred to avoid places where I couldn't roam about as I liked, ordinarily I might have left at this point. But there was nothing waiting for me outside other than the biting cold and the falling snow. Reluctantly, I bought a ticket from her and walked over to the row of hooks to hang up my coat.

The old man, who had finished removing his coat and hat and turned to face me, resembled a retired history professor with his wire-rimmed spectacles and considering that he had come to visit this particular museum, might indeed be one. Judging by the physical resemblance between them, the woman, younger than him by a good twenty-five years, was his daughter. Despite their opting for the English-language tour, it was obvious they were not from the English-speaking world, although I couldn't guess at their nationality.

By the time I, too, was ready, a bearded Finnish guide had already appeared. We walked through a small hall hung with mounted deer and wild goat heads, testifying to an enthusiasm for hunting on Mannerheim's part, and entered a drawing room furnished with glass-fronted, floor-to-ceiling bookcases, comfortable-looking leather armchairs and antique bric-a-brac.

Standing in the centre of the room, the guide said, "Welcome to the home of Marshal Mannerheim" and proceeded to explain how Mannerheim's ancestors had moved in the seventeenth century from the Netherlands to Finland, then a Swedish possession; how they had rapidly prospered in their new homeland, joining the aristocracy with the rank of baron; and how Mannerheim himself, born after the country was seized by the Russians in the nineteenth century, had begun his military career in the Russian Army he would later fight against, and served the Tsar faithfully for thirty years as a high-ranking officer. The English in which all this information was delivered, though, was so heavily accented that, as much because I had difficulty following it, as because of my distaste for guided tours, it didn't take me long to lose interest in the proceedings. Hiding behind the old man and his daughter as best I could, I began studying the heavy carpets on the parquet floor, the oil paintings on the walls, and a silver samovar placed on a polished occasional table in one corner.

The guide was explaining it wasn't unusual for Finns to enter the Russian service in the nineteenth century, and in fact the last governor of Alaska under the Russians had been Finnish.

"I'm sorry," said the old man. "The governor of where, did you say?"

"Alaska," replied the guide. But because he pronounced it "Alusku" as though it were a Finnish placename, the old man had still not understood. I saw his daughter turn to him and, opening her mouth wide, silently form the syllables *A-las-ka*. Then the guide said, "As the dining room is currently being painted, there is nothing else we can see on this floor," and we climbed up creaking wooden steps to the floor above.

Mannerheim's tiny bedroom, entered through the first door on the landing, was decorated in an almost excessively simple style that contrasted sharply with the opulent drawing room downstairs. There was nothing inside other than a low camp bed, an old-fashioned hand-operated field telephone placed on a small table, and a chair with a pair of slippers lying under it. Pointing at the window from which the frozen sea below could be seen through the falling snowflakes, the guide said, "As you can see, the only luxury here is the view" before quickly ushering us out.

Around the room next door stood glass cases containing uniforms Mannerheim had worn at different times in the Russian and Finnish armies. As soon as we walked in, the old man began asking detailed questions about the manoeuvres and tactics employed by the Marshal in, first, the period after the Bolshevik Revolution of 1917, when he broke off relations with Russia and began fighting for Finnish independence, and then twenty years later in the winter of 1941, when he managed to halt the Red Army as it tried to seize Finland back. Once again, I withdrew to one side and began wondering when the tour would end.

It was clear, however, that there was more to see in the museum. After looking at the uniforms we went into a room where Mannerheim's medals were displayed, and when the old man's daughter wanted to know why so many of these incorporated a swastika, I heard the guide explain that this had nothing to do with the fact that Mannerheim had been forced to form an alliance with the Germans during the war: the swastika was a symbol used by Finland long before the rise of the Nazis and indeed still featured in the emblem of the Finnish Air Force.

The woman appeared satisfied with this explanation. After looking at the three of us one by one and deciding no one had any further questions, the guide opened the door of a room equipped with a few rows of chairs and a small white screen at one end, and said, "This last part of the museum could also be claimed to be the most interesting. In 1906, Mannerheim was assigned the task of finding out how big a threat China posed to Russia, and he made a journey to the Far East for this purpose that lasted two years."

I was so astonished by these words that at first I thought I might have misheard him. It was as if, after ensuring I was distracted, he had performed a completely unexpected miracle like a conjuror who, suddenly giving a shake to the crumpled-up handkerchief he has been transferring from hand to hand before the bored audience for minutes, turns it into a fluttering dove. Once again, I couldn't fully follow what the performer of the miracle was saying about Mannerheim's posing as a Finnish scientist to avoid attention on the journey, his travelling to Samarkand by train before crossing the rest of Asia on horseback to reach Peking, and his going on from China to Japan. But I had begun looking at the handful of items displayed in glass cases around the room – the permit issued to Mannerheim to enter China, an English-Chinese dictionary published in Hong Kong in 1895, a pair of binoculars encased in battered leather – not because I was bored but because I was interested.

Mannerheim was not the only traveller to visit the East. Taking advantage of falling airfares and a rising pound, and the fact that the work I did to earn my living didn't have to be carried out at a specific time or place, I had made numerous trips there myself over the last few years. Unlike Mannerheim, I was not on a secret mission. Neither the economic boom which had filled the cities of the Pacific Rim with gleaming new skyscrapers, luxury hotels and consumer goods in the 1970s when America and Europe were stagnating, nor the economic crash that had followed in the 1990s were of much interest to me. Nor was I really interested in the traditional ways of life still surviving in the shadow of the skyscrapers. As usual, all I wanted was to take off, be far away, and lose myself amongst alien sights. In short, I had gone out to the East not because it was the East, but because I was me. But for that very reason I had my own East, and the shape and meaning I had been trying to find in my travels for some time had suddenly started to become clear to me in a museum I had walked into by chance in a city I had come to on a whim.

The guide had switched off the lights and was projecting onto the small screen black-and-white photographs taken both by and of Mannerheim during his journey. For a moment, I looked at the Marshal smoking a pipe under the Chinese willows in the garden of a Buddhist temple, and then walked out of the room and went downstairs, at last able to see how everything fitted together.

The sullen girl was gone; but even if she had been there, I wouldn't have listened to anything she might have had to say about my leaving the museum before the tour was finished. In my mind, this frozen city was already behind me and as I reached for the doorknob I could almost feel the harsh early-morning sun of equatorial southeast Asia on my face once again.

THE PHANTOM DANCE BAND

Welcome to Malaysia.
Despite the words in English above the entrance of the railway station I had been brought to by a Chinese driver through streets just beginning to wake up, I was not yet in Malaysia. Because it had turned out to be cheaper to fly to Singapore, I had done so and spent the night there. But the two countries had a strange, convoluted history. After becoming independent from Britain in 1957, Malaya had united with Sabah and Sarawak in Borneo, themselves former British colonies, and, as if thereby becoming a part of Asia for the first time, had added the name of that continent to its own to emerge as "Malaysia". It had then invited its neighbour, the city-state of Singapore, yet another former British colony, to join the union as well, and when the partnership had not worked and the two parties had separated again soon afterwards, this station built as part of Malaya's railway system under the British had ended up as Malaysian territory.

The pigeons strolling on the empty pavements around the square where the driver had dropped me off suggested the cool of the morning. But as soon as I had stepped out of the air-conditioned taxi, the fierce heat of Singapore had hit me as though an oven door had been opened, and I had begun to sweat.

I put my holdall down and slowly raised my head. With its squat clock tower, low barrel roof and high, narrow windows with carved figures between them labelled "Agriculture", "Trade", "Transport" and "Industry", the station could have been in provincial France. It was as if I was, not at the starting point of one of the most important railways in Asia, but at a town near Avignon or Nîmes where I had alighted by mistake on my way to the Mediterranean.

When I passed through the colonnaded area built in front to create shade and went up the steps, I discovered that, inside, too, there was an air of being in the provinces. There were only four platforms, with, on one side of the departures board (all of the trains listed on which were bound for destinations in Malaysia) a small waiting area serving Platforms 1 and 2, and, on the other side, a similar one serving Platforms 3 and 4. Apart from the closed left-luggage room in one of these areas and the news kiosk in the other, there were none of the facilities to be expected in an international terminus.

When I turned round, I saw, on the wall facing the departures board, the letters KTM, the initials of the Malaysian Railways *Keretapi Tanah Melayu*. The words *Kaunter Tiket* under the initials could only have been derived from the English "Ticket Counter", and, by way of confirmation, there was a row of three booking windows below, of which only the one in the middle was currently open.

Making my way between the rusty iron railings erected to separate those queuing for tickets during busier periods, I approached the old-style opening resembling an upside-down "U" and said to the Malay behind it, "I'd like to take the 8.16 to Kuala Lumpur".

Instead of asking if I was travelling first class or would prefer a window seat, he came back with an unexpected question: "What's your name?"

"Altinel."

"I'm sorry?"

"It might be easier for you to look in there," I said, handing over my passport.

The ticket which he printed and handed to me after propping the booklet open at the page I had pointed out and stabbing at the keys of his battered computer one by one, had on it, as well as my name and my carriage and seat numbers, the Malay version of the greeting in English above the entrance to the station: *Selamat Datang ke Malaysia*. Over the next few days I would discover that the words *Selamat Datang* were everywhere in the country. But what was natural to me was not so much arriving at as leaving a place or, at least, being on the road between two places. Using one of the few Malay words I knew, I mentally converted "Welcome" into "Bon voyage" – *Selamat Jalan*.

The real glory of the station which had struck me as provincial manifested itself when I once again turned towards the departures board to find out the platform my train would be leaving from. In the space between the top of the board and the high ceiling were panels of coloured ceramic tiles depicting scenes from Malay life which looked like they might date from the 1920s or 30s. Peasants dressed in nothing other than a sarong and a turban were tilling the soil with their oxen, and children were shinning up palms to pick coconuts. In plantations, rubber dripped into buckets while native wooden craft with a single sail and the ocean liners of seventy years ago entered harbours.

Between the panels, which had virtually transformed the station into a historic monument in an instant, it was not the letters KTM but rather FMSR that were carved on the wall, presumably for "Federated Malay States Railways". The Federated Malay States was a political entity that had existed in British days. The rajas who had ruled over small independent domains in the Malay Peninsula in the era when Malays were Hindus had begun to be referred to as "sultans" after the country began to adopt Islam as its religion under the influence partly of Arab traders and partly of Indian Muslims;

and the British, who had begun to gain influence over the various sultanates in the eighteenth century, had eventually managed to persuade a number of them to come together as the Federated Malay States while leaving the rest as the Unfederated Malay States. I wasn't certain what the current full name of Malaysia was. As nine of its thirteen states still had a sultan, and every five years these elected one of their number as the overall head of the country, the place I was on my way to might officially be known as the Sultanate of Malaysia.

And the reason for the election of a sultan in addition to the democratically elected state governments and the federal government was the mix represented by the people I joined in the waiting area reserved for Platforms 1 and 2. On the plastic chairs bolted to the floor sat not only Malays but also Chinese, Indians and darker-skinned Tamils. The population of Malaysia was composed of the same ethnic elements as that of Singapore, and although political power was in the hands of the Malays, the economy had always been dominated by the Chinese. One of the measures established to allay the resentment this caused amongst the Malays, who considered themselves "the true owners of the country", was discriminatory laws that reserved state employment for Malays, and another was the sultanate system that was said to "preserve Malay culture". According to the sources I had consulted, the rapid economic rise of Malaysia in the 1970s had reduced inequalities to a considerable extent, and the *Wawasan 2020* programme, launched by the long-term prime minister Dr Mahathir bin Mohamad with the aim of achieving developed-country status for Malaysia by 2020 also promised the simultaneous repeal of discriminatory legislation. As a result, the Malays and the Chinese, who formed the two main ethnic groups, and the Indians and the Tamils, who added to the mix, lived in a greater state of harmony than they had for years, although inwardly they were still not reconciled.

There was no wall at the far end of the waiting area, but a folding grille had been pulled across the gap. Through the spaces in this, empty platforms and motionless lines of carriages could be seen. I sat down next to a woman fanning herself with a folded Chinese newspaper, took out the postcard-sized map of Malaysia I had brought with me from England and began studying it.

Despite regular new arrivals, the occupants of the waiting area could never be called a crowd. When a railway official in a faded blue uniform appeared on the other side of the grille and pushed it open with a creak at around a quarter to eight, they were still sufficiently small in number to arise and move forward as virtually a single body, sweeping me along with them.

Another uniformed Malay sitting in a booth at the gate to the platform briefly flipped through my passport before handing it back. Walking past the silver-coloured carriages, I located my seat in the one immediately in front of the restaurant car, stood aside to let a smartly dressed young Indian pass, placed my holdall on the luggage rack above and sat down.

We left at precisely 8:16 as per the schedule and began making our way through suburbs composed of white blocks of flats in gardens dotted with tropical bushes sporting orange and purple flowers. Although everyone on board was supposed to have entered Malaysia simply by passing through the entrance of the railway station, the actual border crossing was still twenty minutes away, and when we got there, as if to emphasise we were still in Singapore, where Malays couldn't expect preferential treatment, the immigration officers on duty in the exit hall were two Chinese men and an Indian woman in a green sari with a red caste mark on her forehead.

After the last passenger had got their passport stamped and returned to the train, there was a short blast on the whistle and, slowly beginning to move once more, we went out on to the causeway spanning the narrow strait between Singapore and the tip of the Malay Peninsula. Across the water, the ubiquitous "Sony" and "Canon" signs of Asia stood amongst the skyscrapers of Johor Baharu, the principal port of the state of Johor. A bus was moving down the causeway towards Singapore, its windows glinting in the sun, and there were vehicles waiting at a checkpoint to enter Malaysia. But, travelling in our special lane, we crossed the still waters of the strait without stopping and at last reached true Malaysian soil.

At the station, located immediately inland, the platform was full of Malay girls in Islamic headscarves. At one end, two turbaned Malays, identical to the ones on the panels of ceramic tiles except for the shirts they had over their sarongs, squatted, smoking calmly. A little further away, an old man, wearing a woollen suit and a tie despite the heat, was sitting on a bench with a black fez on his head. In the old newspapers and magazines I sometimes looked through, I had seen such fezzes on the heads of young men in yellowing photographs showing scenes from demonstrations against the British presence in Malaya. Perhaps, just as in India there were still members of the Congress Party in white Nehru caps, remembering the days they were imprisoned by the British, there were those here who remembered the days of the United Malay Organisation.

Although the platform was crowded, because everyone was probably waiting for local trains, no additional passengers had joined us. Travelling alongside a dirt road, we picked up speed and passed a row of two-storey buildings, each with a shop on the ground floor provided with shade by an overhanging upper level supported by columns. It appeared that such "shophouses", which I had become acquainted with when I had passed through Singapore for the first time on my way to Australia a few years earlier, were a local feature here on the peninsula as well. Then came more ramshackle low dwellings with television aerials on their roofs.

As if not as big and important as it looked, Johor Baharu had rapidly petered out. Nor were we going to encounter another sizeable settlement for some time. My tiny map indicated that, unlike the road north to Kuala Lumpur, which followed the densely populated coast, the railway traversed the virtually uninhabited interior of the peninsula.

After leaving behind a group of labourers in coolie hats doing something on the muddy bottom of a drained canal, we began travelling amongst wooded hills. Other kinds of trees could be seen here and there as well, but the landscape was dominated by palms: smooth-bodied palms, rough-bodied palms, palms with broad leaves, palms with slender leaves, palms bearing fruit, palms not bearing fruit, palms, palms and more palms. It was a jungle of palms that we had entered.

Such jungle scenery was of course appropriate. I knew that a modern capital city of more than a million inhabitants, with skyscrapers, broad avenues and heavy traffic awaited me in Kuala Lumpur; but, in reality, Malaysia was a tropical country where there were long-tailed monkeys, giant scorpions measuring twenty centimetres, ten-metre-long pythons, "flying snakes" jumping from tree to tree by inflating the pouches on either side of their heads, and even tigers here and there.

Nevertheless, the vegetation I was looking at wasn't entirely natural. There was no doubt that a substantial portion of the palms that stretched away in all directions were wild. But, looking carefully, I could see that many had been deliberately planted in neat rows. Malaysia, amongst whose exports palm oil was almost as prominent as petroleum or timber, had stopped being the giant rubber plantation it had been in British days and become a giant palm plantation instead.

Here and there, rundown houses appeared with corrugated iron roofs that might belong to the labourers working on the plantations. Sometimes there would be a grazing goat or a few scratching chickens or a sleeping dog in front of one of these, but there were no people to be seen anywhere. Again, without either people or a settlement in sight, from time to time a small onion-domed mosque, or a Chinese or Indian temple big enough to hold only a handful of worshippers would pop up by the rails and quickly disappear. Only in places where a red dirt track intersected the railway would I see, waiting at the level crossing, a driver who could be barely made out inside the high cab of his lorry or a rider on a motorcycle who, with his black helmet entirely covering his face, looked like an alien from space that had suddenly materialised in the middle of this strange landscape.

Not only had the scarcity of people not prevented the presence of religious buildings, it had not prevented affirmation of the country's national identity either. Here and there a pole rose on a hilltop, holding up the Malaysian flag resembling that of the United States with a yellow crescent and star on a navy-blue square patch in the upper left-hand corner, and red and white stripes covering the rest of it.

The air conditioning in the train was so efficient that I had been forced to get my pullover from my holdall and put it on. As this didn't prove sufficient, though, from time to time I went out to the section between the next carriage and mine, where there was no air conditioning and, opening the window, I could get an instant blast of soil-and-plant-scented warm air. On one of these trips I had also discovered a pile of that day's English-language *New Straits Times* placed there by KTM for its passengers, and picked one up with the intention of taking a look at it later.

Because I had got up early in the morning and not had breakfast, I was conscious of becoming increasingly hungry.

A little after eleven, I realised I couldn't wait any longer, stood up and, holding on to the backs of the empty seats, made my way down the aisle. I passed the smartly dressed young Indian I had seen earlier and went into the restaurant car.

There was no one inside other than a pair of railwaymen eating in one corner and a Malay in the white jacket of a waiter at the short counter by the entrance. Behind him, a few cans of Coca-Cola and bottles of water stood on the shelves, and on the counter was a line of plastic tubs covered in transparent film containing a dish whose main ingredient seemed to be a long and thin type of noodle resembling bits of string.

Wondering exactly what the dish contained, "What's this?" I asked the man.

"Noodles," he replied briefly.

It was obvious that his abruptness stemmed not from rudeness but a limited command of English. "I have no Malaysian money on me," I said. "Do you take Singapore dollars?"

"Two and a half dollars."

I paid the amount he wanted, picked up the plastic fork wrapped up in a paper napkin he handed to me together with my food and sat down at one of the Formica-topped tables. Although the dish contained the odd piece of vegetable and one or two tiny fish whose spine could be seen through their transparent body, it did in fact consist mainly of noodles. But either because the spicy sauce was well-made or because I was so hungry, the first mouthful I took tasted good. Gazing from time to time at the palms flowing past outside, I went on eating.

A few minutes later, the automatic door of the carriage hissed open, and, raising my head, I saw the new arrival was the young Indian. After standing on the threshold, looking about for a second, he approached me with a smile and said, "Do you mind if I join you?"

"Not at all; please do."

"Are you Australian?"

"No," I said, taken somewhat aback. "I'm Turkish, but I live in England."

"Most foreigners in these parts are Australians; that's why I asked. I am from Bangladesh myself. My name is Ibrahim. Do you know Australia?"

"Not very well, I'm afraid; I've been there only once."

"I went to university there. I was in Brisbane for four years, and now I work for Petronas in KL."

Clearly, just as Los Angeles was referred to as "LA", hereabouts Kuala Lumpur was referred to as "KL". Presumably, the national petroleum company Petronas had been able to employ someone who was ethnically Indian rather than Malay, because he was a foreign national. To show I was taking an interest in what he was telling me, "Is it difficult for foreigners to find work in Malaysia?" I asked.

"Not for those who have a degree from a good university," he said in a tone that was clearly intended to be modest but couldn't disguise his pride.

Just then, the Malay running the restaurant car turned up with a bottle of water for me. The drink, which I hadn't ordered, was clearly his way of apologising for not being sufficiently attentive to me earlier. To help to offset the expense of this gift, I looked at Ibrahim and said, "Would you care for anything?"

But, shaking his head almost angrily, my companion replied "No", and after the Malay had left, bent towards me and explained: "I would have liked a beer, but they wouldn't have anything like that in this place."

He turned his head and looked at the shelves behind the counter as if by staring hard enough he could get a can of Malaysian-brewed Tiger or Anchor to materialise there.

In despair, he then faced me and changed the subject: "Your English is very good."

"So is yours."

"No, you speak like an Englishman."

"I hope the English think so, too."

But he wasn't sensitive to irony. Moreover, he was bored. Like the beerless restaurant car which had prevented him from demonstrating he was a daring consumer of alcohol undeterred by the strictures of Islam, I, too, had disappointed him by not knowing Australia better and allowing him to show how well he knew it, too. Before long, he excused himself and rose, and when I finished my meal and returned to my carriage, I found him sleeping in his seat with his copy of the *New Straits Times* draped over his face.

I sat down and opened my own paper. On the first page, the prayer times for Kuala Lumpur were listed. Ignoring the world news, bad as usual, I turned to domestic news. It was clear that for Malaysia, just as the Chinese were the great enemy within, the Indonesians were the great enemy without. Even the term "Indon" looked less like a necessary abbreviation than a calculated insult; and, according to the paper, Indons were everywhere. Three Indon women had been arrested while trying to enter Malaysia on forged visas; two masked Indons had robbed a jeweller's in Kuala Lumpur, getting away with five thousand ringgits' worth of gold items; transvestite Indon prostitutes operating at a hotel in Ipoh…

Tired of this fear and hatred of Indons, I looked for a while at the advertisements on the back page inviting Malaysians to buy a new Toyota, watch Arnold Schwarzenegger's latest movie, or study medicine at the University of Volgograd. I then folded the paper and put it in the pocket of the seat in front of me.

At ten past twelve we arrived at Gemas. Although the meeting place of the railway running from south to north with the country's second most important railway, running from west to east, the town was little more than a tiny island in the ocean of palms. We rapidly left behind the station with its dazzling pink hibiscuses in big earthen pots on the sunlit platforms, and the handful of broad streets stretching between buildings a few storeys high that followed, and continued on our way.

After this point, the railway began describing an arc that would take it back to the coast. In clearings amongst the palms there now stood traditional Malay *kampongs* made up of brown wooden houses on stilts I was surprised to find still existed. At these places, too, there would be oxen kneeling on the ground or laundry drying on a line between two poles; but, once again, there was no sign of people.

An hour later, finally leaving behind the palms, which had been getting sparser for some time, we came out on a completely flat plain. The fact that Seramban, where we soon stopped, was considerably larger than Gemas was another indication that we were now in a different part of the country.

After that point, towns became increasingly frequent. First would come a small industrial area with timber warehouses and small repair shops; this would be followed by sunny thoroughfares still barely with anyone in sight, and then there would often begin a second industrial area. As we went through one such town, in front of a building, in the middle of whose concreted-over grounds once again a Malaysian flag drooped from a pole, I saw a yellow school bus straight out of American films. I had spent four years in the United States without once seeing such a vehicle, but now there was one here, the traditional inscription in black on its side transformed into *Bas Sekolah*.

Towards two o'clock, I finally saw Kuala Lumpur's skyscrapers towering in the distance above the flat plain. A motorway appeared on the left, followed by tall blocks of flats;

then the skyscrapers approached and surrounded us. We entered a tunnel under them, steadily reducing our speed as we went. At the other end, subterranean platforms like those in an underground station greeted us, and when I turned my face to the windows on the right, the signs outside read: *Selamat Datang ke Kuala Lumpur.*

★ ★ ★

I knew that the central railway station in Kuala Lumpur was one of a number of striking buildings erected by the British that combined elements from Islamic and Western architectural styles. The place we had stopped at therefore had to be an annexe built later. However, at this point what was important was to go and check into my hotel. Deciding to come back and see the station later, I retrieved my holdall from the rack above, and, making my strides as long as I could to restore the circulation in my legs, which had grown slightly numb, stepped out on to the platform.

With trains arriving from other points in the country as well, the escalators were crowded. I found myself a space on a step and went up to the hall above. In exchange for the fifty pounds I handed over, the staff at the "Licensed Currency Exchange", whose sign I had spotted from a distance, gave me a wad of ringgits with a sultan wearing an eye-catching star-shaped decoration in his turban depicted on the front, and modern buildings and vehicles on the reverse of each note. There were taxis waiting under the scorching sun outside. I got into the first one and asked to be taken to Rajah Chulan Boulevard.

Because the economic crisis that had broken out in the Far East a few years earlier had affected Malaysia as well, driving down the value of the ringgit, the road I had named was home to a five-star hotel where I had managed to book a room for a price I would have paid for an ordinary guest-house in England. We pulled out from the kerb into the traffic, which still kept to the left as ordained by the British long ago. True to the country's devotion to its national symbol, many of the vehicles that went by had small Malaysian flags fluttering from their aerials. The skyscrapers along the first road we turned into had been constructed of light-coloured materials to protect those inside from the heat as much as possible. We then turned into other roads with similar skyscrapers; but, Kuala Lumpur being essentially a small city, the trip was brief. Before long, I could see the reflecting-glass-covered bulk of the Hotel Istana ahead.

The driver followed a small private road to the top of the hillock on which the hotel stood and stopped the car. Even before I had finished paying the fare, a young Malay in a canary-yellow uniform had arrived and opened the boot to take my holdall. Together we went inside.

"Istana" meant "palace", and, with its marble floor, its columns covered in tiles with Islamic motifs, and its chandeliers of coloured glass, the lobby could certainly vie with most palaces in gaudiness. Because I had made my reservation through Qantas, the hotel staff, making the same assumption as Ibrahim had on the train, entered my nationality as Australian on the registration form. I signed it without comment, took my electronic room key placed inside a piece of cardboard folded into three with the words *Selamat Datang* on it, and went up to my room on the ninth floor.

In the bathroom there were miniature bottles of shampoo and bath foam bearing the name of the hotel, and in the sleeping area stood an enormous bed and a full-sized sofa. Walking past this nondescript hotel décor, I pulled open the net curtains that covered the large window. On the right, cars could be seen going down Raja Chulan Boulevard, which the side street the room overlooked opened into; and, directly across, two men were playing tennis on a court squeezed in amongst the skyscrapers with an energy that made it hard to believe this was Kuala Lumpur and the temperature was thirty-one degrees. For a moment I looked out, thinking I was once more in a hotel in a city on the other side of the world. Then I went back downstairs and walked out of the revolving door.

During the short time I had been inside, the sun, which had followed me about since the morning, had disappeared. But I knew that in this sort of climate that would make no difference and even with a cloudy sky it would continue to be hot. Hoping that at least the fact that the boulevard went downhill at a gentle angle would prevent me from feeling the heat too much, I walked on.

After making my way between the office blocks on either side for some ten to fifteen minutes, I reached a road that intersected the boulevard at right angles. Seeing that, on the left, the road disappeared under the columns holding up a motorway, I turned right and, within a few hundred metres, was in the old part of the city.

I could now see why there had been so few people in the places the train had passed through. The streets I began turning into at random were crowded enough to suggest everyone in the country had come to Kuala Lumpur. Chinese businessmen with Rolex watches and leather briefcases walked among Malays, most of whom looked, if not poor, of modest means, and short-skirted Tamil girls shared the pavements with headscarved Muslim women in coats coming down to their ankles.

And the vehicular traffic was no less dense. Among the private cars and the lorries carrying goods, buses moved, belching out black exhaust fumes. Since no one seemed to stop at red lights, when I reached a corner I frequently had to wait for a traffic jam to form to cross over.

Most of the buildings I passed were small shops designed to meet the daily needs of the city. But whenever I raised my head, I saw, in the background, the pale skyscrapers against the increasingly murky sky. Like many other Far Eastern cities trying to show how modern they were, Kuala Lumpur had placed amongst the skyscrapers a tower which, with the revolving restaurant and the tall broadcasting mast on top of it, resembled a rocket about to take off. Even more striking was the Petronas headquarters, made up of two identical steel-covered tapering cylindrical towers connected by a bridge in the middle, whose grey silhouette stood in the distance like a pair of giant metal corncobs.

Since, without realising, I had managed to walk for more than an hour in my quest to gain an impression of the city, I had begun to get thirsty. When I spotted a café with round wooden tables on the corner of a broad road, I went in.

Wiping the top of the glass-fronted counter displaying cakes was a Malay in his twenties whose name, according to the plastic tag pinned to the breast of his green uniform, was Ikram. As he handed me the orange juice I requested, "Are you an expat?" he asked.

The word "expat" was something of an expat itself, having started life as the adjective "expatriate" before drifting away from its origins to become first a noun and then an abbreviation. Now everyone who lived or worked in a foreign country was simply an "expat".

"No, I am just travelling," I replied, and was going to continue and explain that I was in Malaysia for a few days, after which I would return to Singapore, but at that point he had to leave me to serve another customer who had walked in.

When I sat down at one of the round tables, I realised why Ikram had thought I might be an expat. Most of those in the room seemed to be in that category. A blond Scandinavian man in glasses was reading a book in Norwegian in one corner, and, judging by their accent, the two women at the next table were from somewhere in the north of England.

After briefly looking me over to see if I was a new addition to the foreign community in the city, one of the women turned to her companion and said: "Roger wants to move to Kelantan because they pay an extra twelve hundred ringgits a month".

"Isn't that one of the sharia states?"

"And how! They have now forbidden even the Chinese to eat pork, and of course there isn't a drop of alcohol anywhere."

"You might as well go to Saudi; at least you'd be making decent money."

"I wouldn't be surprised if we did. The other day I worked out that since 1990 we have spent less than six months in England in all."

Before long the women left the café, and, after sitting a while longer, I too got up to go. It was past five o'clock, but it had started getting dark not because evening was coming but because the clouds in the sky were blacker than ever. Not wanting to be caught in a downpour with nothing on me other than a thin shirt, I decided to go back for my jacket.

By the time, walking past those coming out of the office blocks in Rajah Chulan Boulevard at the end of their working day, I had reached my hotel the first drops had begun to fly in the air. I walked into the Istana which had put all its lights on to counter the gathering darkness and went up to my room. Just as I was reaching for my holdall to get my jacket, as if everything had been waiting for this moment, a flash of lightning filled the large window, and a second or two later, with a deafening crack of thunder, an incredible wall of water began cascading from the sky.

Hoping the downpour would abate soon, I stood ready to leave again; but it didn't show any sign of stopping. The lights of the distant skyscrapers were now blurred behind the curtain of rain, and the tennis court, which the two energetic players, having evidently finished their game, had left, was transformed into a green pond by the water that filled it.

Ten minutes later, realising the rain had no intention of letting up, I turned on the television standing on a shelf on the other side of the bed. But instead of watching the programme in Malay, of which I understood nothing other than the odd word of Arabic or English origin I happened to catch, I contented myself with glancing now and then at its flickering reflection in the darkened window as I continued to look out.

It took me a further twenty minutes to admit that, far from letting up, the rain wasn't going to stop all night; but I was beginning to realise that I was, in any case, too tired from my travelling to go out and do any more walking. Perhaps also because of my tiredness, despite not having had anything all day except the spicy noodles I had eaten on the train and the orange juice I had drunk recently, I wasn't really hungry. I switched the television off and made myself tea, using the electric kettle and the teabags placed on the dressing table. When I finished the cup, I undressed and got into the giant bed, and after listening to the rain outside for a while, fell asleep in a state of exhaustion before it was fully half past seven.

★ ★ ★

When I went out in the morning to begin a more systematic tour of Kuala Lumpur, the private road in front of the hotel and the boulevard below were already completely dry as though not a single drop had fallen from the sky during the night, and the sun and the heat were back in place like stock pieces of stage scenery.

When the headscarved Malay girl who had replaced the young man in canary yellow of the previous day eagerly asked if I would like a taxi, I accepted, thinking I would be doing enough walking during the day. The driver at the head of the rank below, who heard her step out into the middle of the road and clap her hands, started his engine and came up, and we left for the railway station I had decided to see again.

The structure I had seen when I got off the train indeed had to be an annexe added later, because the giant white building at whose gates we shortly arrived looked entirely different. Seeking "an architectural style to reflect Malaya", the British had taken a nineteenth-century rail terminus and placed onion domes, Moorish arches resembling giant keyholes, and towers that looked like minarets with colonnaded balconies all over it. It could of course be argued that colonisers didn't have the right to determine the shape of the buildings to be put up in the countries they occupied any more than they had the right to determine anything else, but, in this particular case, the result was neither unattractive nor out of keeping with the row of palms in front of it.

On the other side of the road, where traffic was light due to the early hour, there was a second, dun-coloured building. Crossing over, I saw a signal of a type used on British railways placed behind the railings as a decoration and discovered from the sign in Malay and English at the entrance that this was the headquarters of KTM.

A short distance away stood the National Mosque built at great expense as soon as the country began to prosper thirty years earlier. But because it had a star-shaped turquoise roof instead of a dome, it was curiously squat and unimpressive. While the British had built a railway station that looked like a mosque, the Malaysians had managed to build a mosque that looked like a railway station.

As I walked on I saw, along the pavements, not only palms but tropical trees of a kind I didn't know, with long feathery fibres hanging from their branches. The crows amongst the leaves, smaller and more hunchbacked than their European cousins and even more wary, eyed me with suspicion; but the yellow-beaked, yellow-footed black mynahs, who, as if trying to prefigure in the animal kingdom the future ethnic divisions of the country, had moved here from India thousands of years earlier, would now and then swoop down, pick up something on the ground and fly away again with the traditional impudence of the starling family to which they belonged.

Before long, I arrived at the huge green *padang* where British teams had once played cricket. Because it had been built for the British rather than the Malays, the Selangor Club at the far end was in mock-Tudor style. As there wasn't even the faintest breeze, the giant flag hanging from the pole, the height of a seven or eight-storey building, erected on the field – now named Merdeka (Independence) Square – was completely still.

Occupying an entire block across the road, the Sultan Abdul Samad Building was the most attractive of the structures dating from colonial times, with its beige brickwork and copper-coloured onion domes. Looking more carefully, I got the impression that the domes were indeed made of copper. The fact that, although slightly tarnished, they had not oxidised to green long ago like the domes I was familiar with in Europe was perhaps due to the climate.

The inscription on the façade indicated that the building, from which the British had administered all of Malaya, now had a more modest function as the *Mahkamah Sesyen dan Majistret Kuala Lumpur*. It wasn't necessary to know that *Mahkamah* meant "court" in Arabic. The other words were even more telling: the British had left behind them their system of dispensing justice through session judges and magistrates, and it was currently the city's law courts that were housed here.

On the corner of Merdeka Square where the road I was following intersected a broader one, there was an artificial tree trunk surrounded by artificial carnivorous pitcher plants of the sort that consumed the insects drowned in the rainwater collected inside them in the country's dense forests. For a while I stood there, looking at the water piped up through the tree trunk drip from the plants above into those below. Then I crossed the road and entered Tunku Abdul Rahman Boulevard, named in honour of Malaysia's first prime minister after independence.

The shop signs along a handful of streets to the right indicated there was a textiles market here, but the premises still had their shutters down. One or two dustmen were picking up the rubbish left on the sunny pavements from the evening before.

About a hundred metres further on, the Coliseum Hotel, where the British owners or managers of remote rubber plantations in the north had stayed once or twice a year when they came to Kuala Lumpur to replenish their stocks of gin and see their Chinese mistresses, was still standing. Like the name of the establishment, the pale pink, blue and green decorative reliefs on the building brought to mind an old cinema in the middle of Glasgow or Birmingham. The warm air stirred by the battered fans on the ceiling hit me in the face as I pushed open the door of the half-dark bar on the ground floor and went in.

There was no one either in the high-backed chairs around the small tables or behind the bar. The walls sported pen-and-ink cartoons of British men with nicknames like "Dinky", "Kinky" and "Stinky" whose watering hole in Kuala Lumpur this had once been. I had read books with humdrum titles such as *Thirty Years in Malaya* or *Memoirs of a Rubber-planter* written by such people in the language of a school essay to describe their lives spent battling with alcoholism, loneliness and the snakes that came all the way up to their houses deep inside plantations.

In the dining room next door, a white-haired Chinese couple were in the middle of an elaborate breakfast consisting of half a dozen different dishes in small bowls. Choosing one of the other tables, all of which were empty, I sat down and began looking around. There was nothing on the off-white walls other than a few decorative plates and large coat-hooks. Reflecting the Asian habit of allowing children of all ages into restaurants, an old metal baby's highchair stood in one corner. On the ceiling, a set of balloons, evidently left from a celebration some weeks earlier and somewhat deflated and puckered by now, stirred in the air currents created by the fans.

A few minutes later, a waiter past seventy emerged from the kitchen, and shuffled over to where I was with a menu. But I shook my head and told him I'd just like some tea.

Although he was clearly unhappy about my not having opted for a full-scale Chinese meal like the two other customers in the room, he went away again without any comment, and, after spending a few more minutes in the kitchen amidst the clattering of pots and crockery, slowly returned bearing a tray with a cane-handled china teapot and a cup on it.

Sipping the refreshing jasmine-scented tea, I took another look at my surroundings. Everything was so old that it was easy to imagine I was a plantation owner sitting here one morning in 1947. Because the ending of the war had reduced demand, the price of rubber was falling, young men in black fezzes had begun cropping up here and there to shake their fists at the British and demand independence, and my friend

Stinky was talking of dropping everything and going to Tanganyika to grow coffee. Then, trying not to wonder why, although I was familiar with so many different ways of life, or at least I thought I was, the only life I could lead was this rootless, drifting one, I finished my tea, paid my bill at the kitchen door to save the trembling old waiter from making another trip, and walked out of the hotel.

The textiles market had come to life, and the shopkeepers, most of whom were headscarved Malay women, were placing their wares on hangers at the entrance to their open-fronted shops. Print tablecloths, tasselled shawls, embroidered blouses and the heat were waiting for me.

After walking down one street filled with textile shops, I turned into a second, at the bottom of which an open-air market resembling a giant pharmacy had been set up under large parasols. The stalls were stocked with bars of soap made of goat's milk, perfumes in tiny bottles, miracle medicines whose potency was attested to by photographs of the horrific wounds they had healed and, here and there, blue packets of Viagra and desensitising creams for delaying orgasm. One or two of the browsers were the sort of sarong-and-turban-wearing Malays I now knew did actually exist. Refusing an offer by a man sitting with a set of old-fashioned medical instruments in a velvet-lined case in front of him to clean my ears for three ringgits, I set out for the space-age Kuala Lumpur Tower.

This was not only further away than I had realised but also on a hill. Pressing on with an obstinacy that left my shirt covered in sweat patches, I reached the bottom of it, but I wasn't in fact really interested in going up to the observation platform immediately below the revolving restaurant. I went through the door, but, instead of joining the queue in front of the lifts, merely strolled through the shops selling souvenirs and postcards. I then sat on a bench in the grounds for half an hour and, looking at the mynahs hopping about in the hope of finding bits of food left behind by visitors, rested there, insofar as it was possible to do so in the heat.

It was approaching half past eleven when, after an even longer walk, I reached Petronas's headquarters standing at one end of a largish square. The steel-covered parts of the twin towers, which, close up, resembled corncobs to an even greater extent with their slightly curved windows, were glinting under the sun. Whether the headquarters, which Prime Minister Mahathir bin Mohamad had commissioned to emphasise Malaysia's determination to achieve developed-country status by 2020, constituted the tallest structure in the world was in dispute, but there was no denying that the profile of Kuala Lumpur, a city of whose existence many people in the world had been only dimly aware of until recently, now stood a little higher as a result of this new piece of architecture. Mingling with a group of schoolchildren brought in a yellow *bas sekolah* to admire their country's success, I lifted my head and, wondering if Petronas's Bangladeshi employee Ibrahim worked in one of these offices with curved windows, I looked for a while at the steel bridge connecting the two towers nearly two hundred metres above the ground.

The small restaurant I found after leaving the business district where the twin skyscrapers were located wasn't very crowded. Taking advantage of this, I lingered over my lunch in order to spend the hottest hours of the day indoors, before taking a bus to the Lake Gardens Park, a short distance from the city centre.

The park, occupying a piece of slightly undulating ground, was left over from the greenery-loving British. The carefully mown lawns, the rhododendrons whose bright colours nearly hurt my eyes under the sun, and the lush flowerbeds filled with orchids and hibiscuses probably attracted hundreds of visitors at weekends, but, on this weekday, there was no one in the area I entered through iron gates.

As I began making my way down an asphalt path, I saw, below, the long and thin artificial lake that gave the park its name, complete with a small palm-covered island in the middle, served by a white wooden humpback bridge on either side. An old man and a little girl who might be his granddaughter were seated on a bench, tossing bits of bread at the crows and the mynahs. I went past them and walked towards three park workers who were trimming some trees with what appeared to be chainsaws.

I was looking for the National Monument, known as *Tugu Negara* in Malay, which I had a vague idea was somewhere in the park. As Malay nationalists had begun struggling for independence in the late 1940s, the Communist Party of Malaya, whose membership was mainly Chinese, had launched its own bid for independence in the form of an armed insurrection, and incidents ranging from guerrilla raids on remote plantations to the ambushing and assassination of High Commissioner Sir Henry Gurney on a deserted road had forced the British to declare a State of Emergency. The colonists had then departed, leaving the country and the Emergency to the Malays, whom it had taken until the 1960s to put the insurrection down. The National Monument, erected shortly afterwards, commemorated this turbulent period.

But by the time I had walked past the park workers wearing beekeeper's veils against the splinters flying in the air and reached the end of the lake I had still not found what I was looking for. A high wall ahead indicated I could go no further. Thinking the monument might be at the other end of the park, which I had entered in the middle, I made my way round the tip of the lake and began walking in the opposite direction.

All I found when I got to my destination, though, was some railings with a busy road beyond them. A few people were sitting in a tea garden on a low embankment, but when I asked them about the National Monument they looked blank and shook their heads. The only one who actually had anything to say was a young man who, seemingly not wanting me to leave completely empty-handed, pointed at the railings and explained, "The Parliament's over there".

Frustrated, I turned into a road leading out of the park and began walking uphill, not really knowing what to do next. At a point nearly halfway up, a Chinese in a t-shirt that said "Golf is Life" was getting out of a Mercedes he had parked by a small lawn. "I am sorry," I said, "Do you know where the National Monument is?"

"Do you intend to walk there?" he asked back in fluent English.

"Yes. Isn't it in the park?"

"No, it isn't: that's why you couldn't find it. Just follow this road and go out, though, and you'll see it ahead as soon as you turn left."

"Thank you for pointing me in the right direction. Perhaps you will allow me to point you in the right direction about something as well?"

"I would be very grateful if you could."

"It isn't life, you know, it's just a game."

He was puzzled for a second, then, realising I was talking about golf, he let out a laugh. "Some might say the same about what you are doing."

"And what's that?"

He shrugged. "Travelling around, looking at other people's monuments."

I left him and walked out of the park. But either his instructions were wrong or I had misunderstood them, for the National Monument was nowhere to be seen. The road

I had turned left into soon split into two. A sign indicated that the right-hand branch went to the Parliament, and the left-hand branch descended towards a motorway where traffic could be seen hurtling towards distant jungle-covered hills that marked the edge of the plain on which Kuala Lumpur stood.

In despair I made for the Parliament to ask there for one final time. But the policeman in a navy-blue uniform guarding the gates gave me the same blank stare as the patrons of the tea garden in the park.

"*Tugu Negara*," I insisted, trying Malay as a last resort. "I would like to go to the *Tugu Negara*."

He looked at me as if to say "Why didn't you say so before?" and declared: "Oh, the *Tugu Negara*? Just turn back and follow this road and you'll find it."

When I failed to reach the monument after walking for a while I was initially not surprised. It was obvious that nobody knew where it was; indeed, it probably didn't exist at all and was just a National Myth. Then, however, I saw a sign ahead on the left that said "*Selamat Datang*".

It appeared that the monument was in a second, much smaller park across from the main one. The Chinese who gave me instructions had perhaps meant that I had to turn left into this park, but failed to mention that, in order to be able to do so I first had to turn *right* when I left the first park.

After walking along a path amongst trees I reached a clearing, from where a longish set of steps led up to a large piece of flat ground. In the middle of this was a U-shaped colonnade whose tips straddled the back edge of a long rectangular pool. A huge bronze sculpture stood here with its back to the colonnade. Four of the thrice-life-size figures, arranged in a manner too similar to the Iwo Jima memorial in Washington depicting the American landings in Japan at the end of the Second World War for the resemblance to be coincidental, were Malay soldiers protected from the sun of their native land by broad-brimmed hats. His left fist raised to the sky, the rearmost soldier was in the act of using his other hand to drive a pole into the ground from which a real Malaysian flag hung. Two of his comrades stood in front of him, their bayoneted rifles pointing forward to defend the flag, while a fourth soldier knelt. There were also three supine hatless figures that the sculptor had probably intended to represent fallen comrades of this quartet, but some might take to represent the defeated enemy.

As it was clear that the victors were Muslim Malays and those they had triumphed over were Chinese, no attempt had been made to use a neutral word like "God" in the inscription on the plinth:

Dedicated to the Heroic Fighters
in the Cause of Peace and Freedom.
May the Blessing of Allah be upon Them.

I wasn't surprised that it should be in this context that I first came upon the name of Allah. It might be strange for a foreigner who had not even spent two full days in the country to come up with such a generalisation, but, despite its headscarved women, its papers listing prayer times, and its sharia states banning pork and alcohol, there was something about Malaysia's espousal of Islam that wasn't wholly convincing. Like the traces left by the British, and the American influence that could be detected in the design of the ubiquitous national flag, the yellow school buses and this sculpture itself, Islam, too, was ultimately a foreign import. The reason it had been more successful than other such imports was because it formed the basis of an identity not shared with the Chinese. For the Malays, their religion, whatever comforts it might provide as a faith, was also a stick to beat the Chinese with.

But perhaps it was better than the actual sticks they had used when they had last taken to the streets thirty years earlier during riots that had left two thousand Chinese dead.

Turning my back on the spot that had been so difficult to find, I slowly made my way across the expanse of raised ground with these thoughts in my mind and went down the steps to the path below. There was a bus stop directly in front of the park, but after ten minutes passed without a bus turning up I began walking towards the skyscrapers of Kuala Lumpur in the distance. Because of the long search I had made for the National Monument, by the time I reached the city centre the copper domes of the Sultan Abdul Samad Building were reflecting the first faint red tinge of the evening sky.

* * *

The next day I bought myself a *dewasa* (adult) ticket at a noisy bus station in Pudu Road and took a *berhawa dingin* (air-conditioned) bus to "Malaysia's historic city of Malacca".

We dropped off the man in the seat in front of me, who had spent the two-hour-long journey shaking his head at the cruelty of fate as he read the death notices in his Malay newspaper, at a market on the outskirts of the city. Then we proceeded to pass timber warehouses and repair shops like the ones I had seen from the train on the way to Kuala Lumpur.

A little past Malacca Hospital, a building resembling in every detail, down to the large Red Crescent emblem on its façade, the hospital in the Anatolian town of Balıkesir we had gone to every year in my childhood to visit relatives, stood a ramshackle restaurant. A headscarved woman and a nurse in uniform eating silently at one of the tables looked preoccupied, as though they were concerned about a patient whose condition was deteriorating. For a second I felt that, as usual,

I was just passing by, constructing stories out of scenes I saw only momentarily (not life but just a game, the Chinese in the park had called it). The mood, though, passed rapidly and I began staring across the muddy river on the right at the rundown houses huddled together under the palms on the opposite bank with curved-prowed native craft moored in front of them.

At the open-air bus station we soon reached there were taxi drivers who had come to meet the bus. I let one of them take me to the hotel he recommended where, for a sum even lower than the one charged by the Istana, I took a room that looked out, over the still, brown river and the low buildings of the city, towards the Straits of Malacca. Above the window that stretched all the way across one wall, a small gold-coloured arrow was pasted on the ceiling. I had to go through most of the information sheets in the leather-bound folder provided for the guests before I discovered it indicated the direction of Mecca for prayer purposes. My curiosity satisfied, I closed the folder and went out.

On either side of the road there were shops hiding under projecting upper floors. Seeing heavy carved cupboards and tables in a number of small carpenter's shops, I was reminded that Malacca was renowned for woodwork. Yellow cakes stood on trays in the window of a Chinese patisserie. A little further on, the owner of an open-fronted shop where grain and spices were sold out of sacks had placed a handful of corn on the pavement for the mynahs. Whether this was an act of charity or a bribe to stop the birds thieving from the sacks wasn't clear.

I could see that the road narrowed ahead to pass between two rows of buildings painted brick red. From the wire strung between the first pair of them there hung an oblong sign saying this was the old part of the city. Malacca's "historic" character was due to its having been seized by the

Portuguese in the sixteenth century when it was the capital of a sultanate grown rich on the spice trade. In time, the city had been taken over by first the Dutch and then the British, with Malaya emerging as a single entity for the first time after the latter had gone on to seize control of the entire peninsula. It was obvious that these red buildings, which, apart from their vivid colour, looked as if they should have been by a frozen canal thousands of kilometres away, were part of the legacy of the Dutch.

Soon I reached a square bordered by a small church, the old Dutch town hall known as the *Stadthuys*, and a clock tower, all of them also painted brick red. Amongst the flowerbeds on the large rectangular traffic island in the middle stood tropical trees, their branches twisted into fantastic shapes as though they were writhing in the heat. Along one side of the island was a line of pedal-driven rickshaws decorated with brass eagles, plastic flowers, coloured beads and of course small Malaysian flags. On the other side of the square, by the river which had emerged from behind the buildings I had been walking past, fruit juice was sold at orange, apple and strawberry-shaped plastic booths.

Ignoring the rickshaw drivers ringing their bells to attract my attention, I went into the church. The interior displayed the freedom from ostentation demanded by the God of Protestantism who wanted His creatures to achieve something in this world instead of preparing themselves for the next through worship. Beyond the empty pews, a large candle rose on either side of the altar, and on the floor, marking the final resting place of Dutch men and women buried inside the church, were slabs, the writing on them eroded by the feet of those coming and going over the last three hundred and fifty years. After taking a brief look at these and at the prayer books and handicrafts at a stall in one corner run by a Christian Tamil, I went out again.

Abandoning its former function, the *Stadthuys* had become the Museum of Ethnography and History. In the glass cases around the rooms on the ground floor, stiflingly hot due to there being neither air conditioning nor ceiling fans, was an eclectic collection of items including everything from china plates and curved Malay daggers to triangular stamps issued at the time the country had gained its independence.

When I left these rooms, which apparently made up the Ethnography section, and climbed up the broad stone steps to the History section, however, there wasn't even such a random assortment of objects waiting for me. As if nothing tangible remained from a five-hundred-year-long stretch of time, the rooms here contained only panels with pictures on them. After pictures of Sultan Mansur Shah, the first notable Muslim ruler of Malacca, and his two famous warriors Hang Jebat and Hang Tuah, there came pictures concerning the *Zaman Portugis* which had begun with the arrival of the Portuguese in 1509. The word *Zaman*, Arabic for "time", then echoed down the centuries as the *Zaman Belanda* of the Dutch was succeeded by the *Zaman British*. The photographs that eventually began to replace pictures on the panels devoted to the latter went on to document the worst of *Zamans*, the *Zaman Jepun* of the Japanese occupation from 1941 to 1945, and then came the *Zaman Darurat* of the Emergency, with the process finally ending with portraits of all the prime ministers who had governed the country since independence, displayed around a room where a row of Malaysian flags hung from the ceiling. At the exit, reached by another set of stone steps, was a "Reading Corner" equipped with an armchair and a small set of bookshelves stocked with past numbers of the blue-covered *Journal of the Museum of Sarawak* and the *Annual Report* of the Central Bank of Malaysia.

By the road that led off from the square in front of the Museum of Ethnography and History, the old British Government House had also been converted and now did duty as the Museum of Independence. Not wanting to be given another illustrated history lesson, though, I just took a look at the two black armoured cars named Hang Jebat and Hang Tuah from Emergency days that were placed outside. Because they were a little too small not just for British servicemen but even for the shorter Malays, they looked like toys, but clearly had once dealt death to Chinese terrorists with the machine guns protruding from slits in their armour plating. A short distance away, under a roof held up by four columns, was an old Chevrolet with tailfins which a sign attached to the railings between the columns said had been bought to take visiting heads of state around during the independence celebrations in 1957. The fact that it had become a museum piece along with the armoured cars seemed to indicate that independence, too, was just a *Zaman* which, like all the others, would eventually vanish. Turning my back on the museum, I walked towards the river.

By the opposite shore, a crane was loading timber from a warehouse onto a craft with a curved prow. Moored just in front of that was a battered white hydrofoil with an inscription on its side promising "Daily Sailings to Dumai". But it had either given up travelling to that Sumatran port in the land of the dreaded Indons across the Straits of Malacca or was at least not sailing that day, because drying clothes hung at its portholes.

Following the road, which turned away from the river at this point, to its end, I found myself amongst office and apartment blocks built on a piece of land reclaimed from the sea. Ahead, the surface of the straits gleamed like a light-blue steel plate, but the nameless new streets forced to wait for the economy of Southeast Asia to improve before the buildings along them could be sold or let were empty under the sun. I walked back and went into an open-air riverside restaurant, which, with the time approaching half past three, was itself empty save for a couple of waiters.

The tables stood in groups of two or three in the shade of long canopies. As I studied the menu with my elbow resting on the railings separating the restaurant from the rocks that fell away to the edge of the murky brown waters, I noticed a dark shadow twisting from side to side as it swam immediately below the surface; but just then a waiter turned up to take my order, and when I looked again, the shadow was gone.

Returning shortly with my beef pilau, "How you find Malaysia, sir?" the waiter wanted to know.

"I find Malaysia hot."

"Not interesting?"

"Very interesting."

Pleased to have got this admission from me, he went away smiling.

Five or ten minutes later, resting after my meal, I saw, out of the corner of my eye, a scaly body on the rocks on the other side of the railings. When I turned round, expecting to see a large snake, a carnivorous monitor lizard, around a metre and a half in length, stood a short distance away. Noticing me, it narrowed its small eyes, turned, and, tasting the air with its forked tongue to find out what lay ahead, slowly went down to the shore where it entered the river. As if to confirm the shadow I had seen earlier, too, had been such a lizard, shortly afterwards, two other monitors came out of the water and began sunning themselves on the rocks.

Deciding to leave the restaurant, I returned to the square with the old *Stadthuys* and the Dutch church that seemed to be the main basis of Malacca's claim to be a repository of Malaya's past. Beyond the plastic fruit juice booths there were once again rundown houses on the other side of the river, but a road carried over the water by a stone bridge could be seen continuing past these ramshackle dwellings into a Chinatown with red paper lanterns. I headed in that direction.

Most of the buildings with faded signs in Chinese were small hotels or antique shops. I spent some time in rooms filled with Buddha statuettes, porcelain vases, cane chairs and ivory carvings. Then, walking past the worshippers amongst the incense sticks burning at an open-fronted temple at the bottom of the road, I turned into a narrow street. There was another temple here with shaven-headed young monks in brown robes. Further away, at a fountain with a row of taps in front of a small mosque, two Malays were performing ritual ablutions prior to going inside to pray. Realising there was nothing left in the city I could see, I went back to my hotel to wait for the evening.

When I went out again several hours later, a thick tropical darkness had fallen. As I walked through the small square with the old Dutch church I couldn't help wondering if, the way foxes came into suburban gardens in England at night, monitors roamed the streets here. But the silhouettes I could make out ahead belonged only to rickshaw drivers still waiting for a fare. Dim lights reminiscent of a wartime blackout burnt in the rundown houses by the river and a sound like static from a giant radio rose from the tens of thousands of insects in the trees. The red lanterns of Chinatown were lit, but because the shops were closed, the area looked dark and deserted. I ate the last dinner I was to have in Malaysia in a small bar with half a dozen tables. When I came out, a distant, tiny relative of the monitors, a ten-centimetre-long gecko was using the suction pads on its feet to climb the rough white wall of the house opposite in search of its own dinner. Listening to the indecipherable, rising and falling message of the insect chorus, I walked away.

* * *

Singapore, which had struck me as cold and rigid when I passed through on my way to Australia, made an entirely different impression on me on my return from Malaysia. Glimpsed from the window of my bus, the well-kept boulevards under the afternoon sun, the orderly traffic, the students in uniform in front of the Chinese Girls' High School with its founding date (1899) and motto (Honesty, Courage, Generosity, Service) inscribed on its perimeter wall, now appeared to me not cold and rigid, but mild and orderly.

Stronger economically than Malaysia, Singapore had managed to get through the economic crisis affecting the region without its currency losing any of its value. As a result, I was once again booked at the hotel in Little India I had chosen last time for being cheaper than the other big hotels in the city. Going up the white steps in the heat that made it clear that I was now even nearer to the Equator, I entered the spacious lobby I remembered.

"If you don't know Singapore I can lend you a guidebook," said the man checking me in.

"I was here a few years ago."

"In that case you may not need a guidebook, but I am sure you'll still find a lot has changed in that time."

When I went out to look around, I discovered he was right. The city, constantly trying to be more modern, had indeed changed. Most of the shophouses had been replaced by new buildings or, worse, renovated and turned into luxury restaurants and boutiques. The city buses ventilated by the slipstream entering through their unglazed windows fitted with horizontal bars, which could still be seen here and there amongst vehicles with proper air conditioning on my first visit, were no longer around. Even the monsoon drains with metal covers by the pavements that had interested me so much had disappeared, as though a new method had been found to deal with this problem.

But none of this was sufficient to lessen my newfound affection for Singapore. In any case, not everything had changed. On a piece of wasteground off Kampong Kapor Road there still was a ramshackle street market offering bizarre used items such as rusty keys, telephone cards with no credit left in them and electric irons that didn't work. The statues of angels guarding the tombs in the overgrown yard of the Armenian Church built in the nineteenth century were still on duty. Just off Orchard Road, resembling a tropical Champs-Élysée with its big shopping centres and crowded pavements, the hundred-year-old grey-and-white Goodwood Park Hotel was still standing.

After spending the afternoon taking in these familiar sights, as evening was approaching, I went to take a look at the river passing through the city's main business district. Making its way between the skyscrapers housing the Singapore branches of international banks and investment houses, the broad green waterway flowed towards a bridge with spherical white lamps resembling giant table tennis balls on either side. A quarter of a century ago, I had left behind another green river whose course between skyscrapers took it under another bridge with exactly such lamps in Chicago, and never gone back.

I crossed over and entered a street by the water at the foot of the skyscrapers that was lined with small bars and restaurants. It was that time of the day when, as if darkness were something that rises from the ground, dusk begins to gather down below, although there is still light in the sky. Young expats who had finished their day's work in the offices in the area were seated on stools in front of a pair of adjacent bars, watching on big television screens a football match that had been played in Europe the evening before. Further away, Singaporeans were already eating at tables placed outside Chinese and Indian restaurants.

Instead of joining the diners, I walked up to the end of the street and crossed back by another bridge to the opposite bank, which was almost deserted as it didn't have restaurants along it. In a small square a short distance away, a white statue of Sir Stamford Raffles, the East India Company official responsible for purchasing uninhabited Singapore Island from the Sultan of Johor and founding the first settlement on it at the beginning of the nineteenth century, was gazing back at a handful of Japanese tourists gazing at it.

In the road I reached by walking round the back of the statue, a rare breeze was stirring the Singapore flag on the dome of the High Court left over from the British. The first example of its kind I had seen because of Singapore's more sparing display of such symbols than Malaysia, the flag consisted of a white lower half and a red upper half, with a crescent and five stars arranged into a pentagon in the top left-hand corner. I remembered reading that the crescent represented the rise of Singapore, and the stars stood for Democracy, Peace, Progress, Justice and Equality; but, with their associations with Islam, these symbols also seemed to have been chosen to appease the Malays and the Muslim Indians who, although in the minority here, still constituted an important group.

Flanked by a cricket field even bigger than the one in Kuala Lumpur, this thoroughfare, too, was virtually deserted, but, at the bottom of it, dense evening traffic flowed past the skyscrapers along Bras Basah Road which were now brilliantly lit. After waiting at a crossing with law-abiding Singaporeans for the lights to turn green, I reached the other side and walked for nearly another hour to get back to Little India.

I was now hungry enough to eat something somewhere myself. But the sawdust-sprinkled stone floor and plastic tables of the C.M.K. Restaurant offering "Exceptional Muslim Dishes Twenty-four Hours a Day" in Syed Alwi Road didn't really appeal to me. Walking past the gold rings and chains glittering in the windows of the jewellers filling the Mustafa Centre (the word had not been spelt "Center" in the American way – Singapore was still British) under the Mustafa Hotel, I turned into Serangoon Road.

Although there was more than a month to go until Diwali, the great Hindu Festival of Light, large cutouts of elephants and candles were attached to lampposts. The shops with bolts of cloth piled up outside them I had seen the last time I was here had reminded me of the shops in the Turkey of my childhood. They had since been torn down, leaving a large empty lot across the way, but an Indian restaurant next to this had survived the destruction and was inviting custom with the fairy-lights flashing in its windows. I had found the place to eat that I wanted.

The fact that everyone inside was Indian seemed like a seal of approval, but because most of the tables were occupied, the service was rather slow. I had to wait a long time for my chicken curry, and although when it finally arrived it justified the clientele's vote of confidence in the cooking, there was too much of it for me to eat by myself. Despite having been made still hungrier by my wait, it didn't take me long to start feeling full. I pushed away my plate and began looking at my fellow-diners.

At the next table two men with dark moustaches, brothers perhaps or business partners, were sitting with their wives. The men were dressed in pale shirts, and the women, who were in saris, wore small earrings made of what looked like genuine precious stones. Behind them, there was a large family group who seemed to be celebrating an occasion like a wedding or a graduation; and a little further away, an old man sitting with his wife was dextrously rolling his food into a ball with the fingers of his right hand before taking it to his mouth.

Then, at a table by the far wall, I spotted a somewhat chubby but handsome boy of sixteen or seventeen eating with obvious pleasure while simultaneously talking to three girls of around the same age as him who were listening in rapt attention. He was someone whose entire future could be seen at a glance. He would always enjoy himself, always effortlessly be attractive to women, and fill his days with flirtations, trysts and happy, relaxed post-coital naps. Did one need to be attractive to women in order to be happy? Or was it, as some thought, fame or money that was needed? I myself had only wanted to see the world and to write about my experiences, but I was no longer sure where those two ambitions had brought me.

I shrugged and looked away. There was no point in having such thoughts by an empty lot in Serangoon Road. The owner of the restaurant, having seen I hadn't finished my chicken, was hovering about in some anxiety: I assured him the amount I had left uneaten was only due to the generous helping, paid the bill and walked out.

The night outside was entirely different from the dark night, silent except for its cacophonous insect chorus, that had greeted me twenty-four hours earlier in Malacca. The hum of a big city penetrated even into this somewhat remote corner of Singapore, and outside the Mustafa Centre there were men talking loudly in Hindi at payphones. I thought of going to have coffee somewhere, but I changed my mind, turned right at the corner and walked towards my hotel a hundred metres away.

★ ★ ★

When I opened my eyes on the last day of my trip, a Saturday, I already knew where I would be going. At the beginning of the Second World War, Singapore, then still a major trading post of the British Empire, had begun awaiting the arrival of the Japanese Navy and acquired the reputation of an impregnable fortress with its giant guns trained on the sea. But, instead of confronting those guns, the Japanese had landed in the north of Malaya, and, driving their small tanks round the rubber trees in the plantations and making their way through the jungle on bicycles, had seized the entire peninsula with a speed which had brought them to the gates of Singapore within one month. Despite a cable from Churchill saying it must be held at all costs, the city had fallen after two weeks of street fighting, and along with local troops, 120,000 men sent as reinforcements from Britain, India and Australia had been taken prisoner. The Japanese secret police, the Kempeitai, had then turned the Goodwood Park Hotel into their headquarters, and the conquerors, who claimed they were fighting to liberate Asia from the Western yoke, had begun torturing and murdering their Asian brethren with some enthusiasm. Today, neither those who came to the city on business or to shop, nor the city itself seemed to take much interest in any of this, but, under the calm and orderly surface of Singapore, one or two traces from the past still survived.

By now largely used to the heat licking my face, I slowly made my way to the city centre on foot. The cenotaph erected after the First World War, which had struck me with its large contingent of Scottish names on my first visit to Singapore, now attracted my attention for a different reason. On each of the five steps leading up to it was carved the date of one of the five years of the war from 1914 to 1918. When the other side of the monument had later been used for the Second World War, however, five steps had proved insufficient, and the dates 1944 and 1945 had been carved on the stone body of the cenotaph itself. Above these was a list of names, some of which were once again Scottish, but there was nothing to indicate who the handful of individuals on the list were or why, out of the thousands that had died, they alone had been chosen for commemoration here.

Walking past a concert hall under construction on the right, I reached a small park a short distance away. Here there was a taller memorial to the 50,000 civilians the Japanese had managed to kill in the space of four years. I knew that the urns around the four tapering pillars, so close to each other as almost to form a single obelisk, contained the ashes of some of the dead. On the base was a brief inscription in English indicating the nature of the memorial, accompanied by what must be translations in Chinese, Hindi and Malay. I couldn't read the Chinese or the Hindi alphabet, but the passage in Malay contained the words *Zaman Jepun* I remembered from the History Museum at Malacca.

I left the park and continued on my way. The two monuments I had seen might not arouse much interest, but, being at the city centre, they had a chance of being noticed by someone from time to time. What I really wanted to see was the large war cemetery which Singapore had pushed to the other end of the island as if suppressing a painful memory. I bought a ticket at a nearby underground station and boarded a train full of young Chinese in white t-shirts, reading textbooks on electronic engineering and information technology.

Kranji, which the train took nearly forty-five minutes to reach after rapidly emerging overground and stopping at platform after sunny platform amongst high-rise collective housing, was one of the last stops on the line. When I got out of the carriage, by then almost completely empty, I was greeted not by a built-up area but rather a busy road bordered by market gardens and clumps of trees. Taking advantage of the fact that there was at least a pavement, I walked on a little and spotted the cemetery draped over a low green hill ahead.

At the entrance, reached by a narrower thoroughfare that left the road and began to climb gently, there was a bus with a sign placed against its windscreen that indicated it was chartered by a group of war veterans from Melbourne. The fact that the veterans had come to Singapore instead of going to Thailand suggested that they had been not amongst the prisoners of war taken north by the Japanese to build the "Railway of Death" to Burma, but the troops the Australians had managed to withdraw from the island at the last moment.

In the middle of the cemetery there was a broad grass strip, and identical white tombstones climbed up the hill on either side in neat rows. A giant cross stood almost at the summit, and behind it there was a monument consisting of thirteen parallel walls with a flat roof over them. Because the wall in the middle continued above the roof, the structure looked like the tail of a giant aircraft.

I began walking amongst the graves in the deep silence of the cemetery disturbed only by a bird bursting into song somewhere now and then. Most of the dead whose names and serial numbers appeared in the front rows were from the Australian forces. But, slowly, the names of British military units – the Surrey Regiment, the Hertfordshire Regiment, the Leicestershire Regiment, the Manchester Regiment – began to mingle with these. Like the size and shape of the tombstones, the inscription they bore, too, was identical in most cases: "His Duty Done, Ever Remembered". There was, though, the odd variation. The cross carved on each tombstone was accompanied here and there by the winged emblem of the British or the Australian Royal Air Force. A young officer had fallen asleep "Till the Day Dawns and the Shadows Flee Away", and a military doctor had died not "For God and Country" in English but *Pro Deo et Patria* in Latin.

The cemetery was so big that it had swallowed up a busful of Melbournian ex-servicemen and their wives. I only saw one or two of them from time to time amongst the white headstones. But eventually they began trickling down the grass strip in the middle in small groups to return to their bus. Amongst those going down, an old man in a straw hat stopped by me and, gesturing at the graves, said, as though we were two strangers talking in a corner at a crowded party, "Is there anyone you know here?"

"No, there isn't," I told him. "I'm Turkish."

"I've got a friend a little further up; we were here together when the Japanese came. How I got away myself, I'll never know; there can't have been such a badly managed campaign in history: the man in charge should have been court-martialled."

"Do you mean Percival?"

"Yes, I do; but to be honest, Bennett wasn't much better. If you know about Percival, you must know about Bennett, too."

I did. Like A. E. Percival, commander-in-chief of the British and Empire forces in the Malay Peninsula, Gordon Bennett, commander of the Australian contingent, had managed to escape a court martial, but history had not been altogether kind to these two men who were perhaps guilty of little more than having to make difficult decisions in complicated circumstances. Percival, in particular, seemed destined to be remembered by the photograph showing him marching with a white flag in his hand to surrender to General Yamashita at the latter's headquarters just outside Singapore.

But, although the words used by the old Melbournian were bitter, his tone didn't carry any real anger. I realised that he wasn't, as I had hoped for a moment, going to tell me about the air raids on Singapore: the black smoke that covered the sky as the rubber godowns stuffed with the wealth of Malaya burnt, the last ships that arrived to evacuate the women and children to England and the young soldiers who, despite everything, went on swaying with the taxi dancers in their arms at establishments like The Great World. Death, which, sixty years ago, had detained his friend and let him go in Singapore, would, any day now, call for him, too, in Melbourne, and with the indifference brought on by the knowledge of that fact, he no longer had much to say to anyone. When his bus hooted from down the hill shortly afterwards, he left me and walked away.

Left alone on the slope after I heard the bus start its engine and drive off, I walked slowly towards the summit. On the walls of the monument were inscribed the names of 24,000 individuals who had been killed not only in the fighting in Singapore but at various locations in this corner of Asia, but due to wartime conditions had not received a proper burial. And on the other side of the hill, with their backs turned to the giant cross, Hindus and Muslims lay in graves which, once again, were identical. Members of the Hyderabad Regiment, the Indian Army Ordnance Corps, the Brigade of Gurkhas and the Federated Malay States Volunteer Forces were here.

I left the cemetery with the hollow feeling that an encounter with death always brings, exacerbated by the guilt of having turned even the dead into objects of sightseeing, and, as if to punish myself, decided to walk all the way back to Singapore. It didn't take me long to lose my way amongst nearly identical high-rises, and although I eventually recovered my bearings, I got lost several more times along the way, as well as making a number of pit stops at cafés to rehydrate myself. By the time I finally reached my destination, dusk was already falling and a sliver of a moon straight out of the Singaporean flag hung in the luminous royal blue sky.

Still full of nervous energy, I headed, without quite knowing why, for the Raffles Hotel, restored, after long neglect, to its nineteenth-century glory some years earlier for the benefit of millionaire tourists and business travellers spending someone else's money. The light from the chandeliers burning inside the three-storey white building fell on the garden outside. I stood for a moment and looked at the imposing entrance, the ornate window frames, and the letters spelling out the name of the establishment immediately below the roof; then I went round the corner into the courtyard at the back.

Here, there were two rectangular bars of the sort where the barman serves from the space in the middle. There was nobody round the one at the far end of the courtyard, but a mixed group of English expats in their thirties sat drinking round the one near the entrance. As it was still early, neither the dancefloor between the two bars nor the small stage built for the band was in use. But because the hotel's sound system was excellent, a dance tune from the 1920s, dominated by a piano and wind instruments, filled the courtyard with a vividness that suggested a real band.

Listening to the music, I slowly climbed a set of stairs with a broad banister, walked down a corridor from where the courtyard below could be seen through open arches, and reached the famous Long Bar. The door was ajar and those sipping expensive cocktails inside could be heard talking in hushed voices as though awed by their surroundings. A waiter who appeared at the other end of the corridor stared at me as if he was aware that, even though I could stuff my pockets with ringgits and afford to go anywhere I pleased in impoverished Malaysia, I wasn't the sort to make an appearance at places like this in Singapore; but he walked past without comment.

As I was going down to the courtyard again, I saw another waiter behind the bar at the far end lighting the candles on a birthday cake and I realised what the English expats had come here for. When a tiny flame appeared at the tip of the last candle, the waiter placed the cake on his right palm, carried it across the dancefloor, causing the flames to be swept back, and, with a deft flourish, put it down in front of a young woman sitting with her back to him at the other bar. At the same moment, the fake trombones of the sound system stopped and, in the sudden silence, those round the bar began to sing "Happy birthday to you! Happy birthday to you! Happy birthday, dear Louise!"

Louise clapped her hands like a little girl at this surprise and, flinging back her red head, let out a drunken laugh. But in the gathering darkness her eyes were strangely dull by the trembling light of the candles. Looking carefully, I could see that most of the expats had the same vague listlessness underneath their cheerful appearance. It was as if they suspected they had made an irreparable mistake somewhere. For a moment I felt like telling them that this couldn't be true, that England was only thirteen hours away, and they could always go back and start afresh if they wanted. But maybe I was wrong: maybe they had long ago fallen under the spell of the music played by phantom bands in foreign hotels, got used to living in other countries amongst other people's lives, and reached the point where they could no longer return anywhere. And maybe I wasn't so different from them either.

CAFÉ SAFARI

There were flat, green islands here and there in the South China Sea. I was one of the few passengers in the First Class section of the jetfoil skimming the wavetops on its way to Macao like a low-flying aircraft. Since leaving Hong Kong half an hour earlier, we had been travelling in busy waters filled with freighters, tankers and the odd barge loaded with crates of fruit and vegetables or chickens in cages.

Although it was early December, there was still some watery sunlight, and mild days to match, in this subtropical region. On the Sunday evening I had arrived in Hong Kong, the women chatting on benches in the dark under the bauhinia trees with their pink and purple flowers in Chater Garden had reminded me of summer. Later, though, I had found that, sometimes early in the morning or as evening closed in, the temperature would suddenly drop and winter would make an appearance in the city like a visitor from far away.

Hong Kong, handed by the British back to China, but, instead of being integrated into that country, turned into a "Special Administrative Region" with the promise that everything would be kept the same for fifty years, was, to all appearances, much as it had always been. On the roofs of official buildings, the Union Jack had been replaced by the red Hong Kong flag with a white bauhinia flower on it which, as befitted a place that was not an independent country but only a "region", was a mere two-thirds the size of an ordinary national flag. But the companies set up by the old British families mainly from Scotland – the Jardines, the Mathesons, the Swires – who had managed to turn an uninhabited rocky island seized from China during the Opium Wars of the nineteenth century, and a few hundred square miles directly across from it on the mainland, into one of the world's important cities, were still there. Street signs and destination boards of buses, too, were full of names of Scottish origin, written in both the Chinese and the Latin alphabets – Edinburgh Place, Argyle Street, Dundas Street, Bute Street, Findlay Road, Aberdeen. Preserving its complex Anglo-Scottish-Chinese identity, Hong Kong was involved in a ceaseless rush with its impressive skyscrapers, its pavements almost too crowded to walk on and its overhead walkways straight out of Fritz Lang's *Metropolis*.

I had wandered through the city at random without making a special effort to see any particular part of it. Every morning I left my hotel in Kowloon on the mainland and, looking at the shops on the ground floors of fifty-year-old office blocks festooned with signs in Chinese, walked to Tsim Sha Tsui. Then, to be able to gaze at the striking view of the skyscrapers serried along the edge of Hong Kong Island, I crossed over, not by underground under the harbour, but by one of the green-and-white vessels known generically as the "Star Ferry" because of the word "Star" forming part of the name of each of them. On the island itself, the old double-decker trams made by the English Electric Company took me to Kennedy Town or Causeway Bay to saunter about amongst shops, seafood restaurants, and cafés with wide-open windows where old men slammed down their tiles as they noisily played mahjong.

When I went to a café myself at noon and opened the *South China Morning Post*, still published in English, editorials, which had never needed to express any worry about British intentions, nervously asked exactly what China intended and how much longer Hong Kong's freedoms would really remain intact, although the financial pages still invited foreigners to invest in the city. I then folded my paper, finished my meal and walked for several more hours before sometimes taking a bus that followed a circuitous route and sometimes the direct funicular to Victoria Peak. I stood there, looking down on the skyscrapers, now serene and silent at the bottom of the vast, wooded slope, the ships in the harbour and distant Kowloon, before making my way down again to pass through Wan Chai with its small bars and nightclubs in the gathering dark.

When I returned to my hotel late at night, I always found someone had made my bed, and, turning down one of the top corners of the covers, left on the pillow a message saying "Tomorrow the temperature in Hong Kong will be between 18 and 22 degrees Centigrade. We wish you a pleasant stay" together with two chocolates wrapped in green foil. I ate the chocolates, wrote my notes on the day and then went over to the window to gaze at the Chinese lives whose texture and meaning I didn't know, unfolding in the lit rooms of the twenty or thirty-storey blocks of flats across the road, as though I were gazing at a text in Chinese I'd never be able to read.

After spending five whole days in this manner, I had decided on the sixth to go to Macao on the other side of the Pearl River estuary, which, after centuries as a Portuguese colony, had quietly become another Special Administrative Region of China only a year earlier. Because it was already quite late when I had this idea, by the time I had made the necessary arrangements for returning to my hotel the next day and got myself to the jetfoil terminal, it was almost half past two in the afternoon. But as the service was quite frequent, and most of those who travelled from Hong Kong to Macao were Chinese flocking at weekends to casinos at the latter location where, unlike in Hong Kong, gambling was allowed, I had had no difficulty finding a seat on this weekday.

I turned away from the window and picked up the form the stewardess, who made the jetfoil seem even more like an aircraft, had put down in front of me a minute earlier. The fact that, as with Hong Kong, even Chinese citizens needed a passport to enter Macao, and the entry form that had to be completed was still printed in Chinese and Portuguese gave the impression that, for the time being at least, the official handover had not changed things here much either. I put down my first and last names in the section marked *Nome completo* and my passport number in the one marked *No de documento de viagem*, and hesitated for a second over *Ocupação* before choosing for myself the designation *Escritor* (writer).

By the time I had finished filling in the form, Macao could be seen in the distance. Although it was often said that because Portugal, a world power at the time it had acquired Macao in the sixteenth century, had subsequently declined, the colony had remained underdeveloped – and, therefore, possibly also more interesting – compared to Hong Kong, a handful of postmodern skyscrapers that could be seen along the shore seemed to speak of a new spirit of enterprise. Then everything slowly got nearer and larger, and I saw the pale blocks of flats climbing up the hills behind the skyscrapers. We passed under an extremely long bridge linking Macao to the island of Taipa, a part of the former colony, turned to starboard and docked at a terminal flying the little green Special Administrative Region flag of Macao with a white lotus and five yellow stars on it.

Although not many passengers had arrived from Hong Kong, there were noisy tour groups off ships from mainland China inside, filled with the excitement of leaving their country for the first time. The Macanese immigration officers spent a long time interrogating their Chinese brethren, whom they seemed to regard with a degree of contempt. When it was my turn, however, my passport was promptly stamped and returned. As soon as I left the arrivals hall, resembling its counterpart at an airport in a way that continued the air-travel motif, a black taxi with a cream roof appeared and stopped in front of me. I got in and asked to be taken to the Hotel Lisboa, the only place to stay I knew of in Macao.

The hotel, which we reached quickly after driving down a road with a few office blocks and shopping centres, was at one end of a large circular plaza with an imposing fountain in the middle and a second bridge leading to Taipa at the other end. The orange-and-white cylindrical building with an aura of having been built in the 1950s had a strange white roof with curved edges, perhaps designed to bring Chinese architecture to mind, but in fact reminiscent of neither that nor any other established architectural style. A gold-coloured decoration in the shape of a cut diamond was erected on top of the roof, and around this were gold-coloured bars ending in a sphere like giant pins. Next to the main building was a four-storey orange-and-white casino that looked like a smaller replica of it, and behind this pair rose an annexe which was also orange and white but square in shape. I got out of the taxi, walked past the Chinese doorman who, to guard this establishment bearing the name of Portugal's capital, had donned the wide-brimmed hat, short burgundy jacket and tight trousers of a Portuguese bullfighter, and went in.

Everything from the doors of the lifts to the buttons on the uniforms of the staff was new and shiny. But because it was a weekday, room rates had dropped sharply. Offered a room with a harbour view on the twentieth floor of the annexe that normally went for 2,000 Macanese patacas for a mere 750, I took it and went up. I could see from the picture window that there were neon signs on the roofs of the main building and the casino which were unlit at this hour.

For a few moments I looked at these, the giant golden pins, the grey and dull sea stretching away under the winter sun outside, and the cars moving towards Taipa on the long bridge; then I turned my gaze to the interior of the room. On the dressing table lay the thick, bound *Casino Guide* issued by the local Gaming Board, the *Sociededa de Jogos de Macau*. But I hadn't come here to gamble. I went downstairs again to go out and see the city.

In a road leading off the circular plaza the hotel was located by, a pink colonial building with white columns stood in a garden filled with palm trees. A framed menu hanging outside indicated it was now a restaurant, but on its façade there was an inscription in black letters that showed its original function had been different:

Clube Militar
1870.

A hundred years ago, as Europe prepared for a new war, young Portuguese officers with golden epaulettes had probably walked under these palm trees, smoking their after-dinner cigars in the dark and telling each other everything was about to change. Looking at the harp-shaped relief above the black lettering and the old-style globes composed of iron hoops placed inside one another, on either side of the three short flag poles on the roof, I thought this prediction had proved both right and wrong. Everything had indeed changed, if not with that war, then over time, leading to the shattering of the iron hoops with which the old imperialists had bound the world; but the slavery of the slaves had merely continued under different masters.

I walked along the road, following the moderately dense traffic made up of elderly cars, motor scooters steered by helmeted drivers, and battered orange municipal minibuses.

Then I came to a fork and took the narrower and less busy road on the right.

Because, as in Hong Kong, here, too, a large number of people had to live in a small area, there were blocks of flats of twenty, thirty and sometimes even more storeys on either side. But these were rundown structures compared to the ones I had been seeing for days. Their paintwork was faded and the air conditioning units at their windows were rusty. I could see drying laundry, flowerpots and plastic water butts on balconies completely encased in railings which, because burglars could hardly operate at such heights, had to be there to prevent those inside from falling out, rather than to prevent anyone from getting in.

In the slight gloom that pervaded the area at this late hour of the afternoon, the small shoe shops and outfitters under the blocks displayed the same air of stagnation with their dusty windows and outdated wares. Because this was the atmosphere I had always encountered in Portugal, too, it felt as if I was in the back streets of Lisbon. But the trees along the pavements were not the usual European varieties but tropical banyans which, because of their way of not being content with their subterranean roots and sending down dozens of additional ones from their trunk and even their branches, had turned into untidy brown bundles.

A little further on, next to a small sports field on the right where a group of sweating Chinese children were playing football amidst much shouting, there was an arrow-shaped sign with the word *Parque* on it at the bottom of a street climbing at a sharp angle. Holding on to the handrail by the kerb across from the sports field, I began pulling myself up towards the trees I could see at the top.

Entering the park, which the map at the gates indicated to be sizeable, I encountered another sign that said *Farol da Guia*. I had no idea what this meant, but the little picture of a lighthouse next to the words had intrigued me. Following a small, deserted gravel path, I climbed a little further and, at the highest point of the hill, found a squat white lighthouse similar to the ones I had seen on the rocky Atlantic coast of Portugal. It looked as if it had been built centuries earlier and restored several times since then, but it wasn't clear whether it was still functioning. One of the long bridges leading to Taipa and the grey silhouette of the island could be made out in the distance, and on the right I could see, through the entirely still leaves of the trees, the pale buildings of the city spread out below, one or two of them topped with a green Special Administrative Region flag. Everything was distant and silent as the day prepared to end.

I left the area at the bottom of the lighthouse and made my way back down the hill to the road I'd been following before I spotted the sign for the park. At this point there were one or two imposing colonial villas, and past them there was a public Chinese garden surrounded by a yellow wall. I walked up to its gate topped by a roof with curved edges, and glanced inside at the winding paths between artistically arranged rocks in curious shapes, the bamboos with slender leaves, and the people sitting on benches with colourful tropical birds in cages by them which they seemed to have brought out for a breath of fresh air as though they were dogs needing a walk. But, instead of going in, I pressed on and turned into a cobblestone street where there was now even less daylight because of the late hour.

After the street made its way for a while between small, nondescript jewellery and grocery shops, the flank of a hill appeared on the left, and, taking a few more steps, I found myself in the small square where the ruined façade which was all that remained of the São Paulo Cathedral built by Portuguese Jesuits in the sixteenth century, and familiar to me from photographs, stood. Under the stone dove representing the Holy Ghost at the very top of the ruin, real doves and pigeons heedless of the handful of strollers in the square were preparing to settle down for the night in the niches made to house statues of saints.

The streets at the bottom of the broad steps leading down from the ruin looked as if they were about to fill with darkness. But when I saw a path leading up to an old Portuguese fort on top of the hill on the left, hoping to be able to take a look at this building as well before the sun set, I quickly climbed to the top, struggling for breath.

There was a large iron plaque with raised lettering on it, sunk into the massive stone wall of the fortress. Over the years, both the plaque and the wall had darkened and become nearly indistinguishable from one another, but the inscription *Sentido! Recorda por uns Instantes a Historia da Nossa Patria!* could still just about be discerned. Relying on similar English, Latin and Italian words I knew, I construed this as best I could: "Feel it! Remember for an Instant the History of Our Homeland!"

All that was left of "the history of our homeland" inside the fort was a set of ancient bronze cannon pushed into the crenels in the battlements. But because this hill, although not as high as the one the squat lighthouse was located on, was closer to the harbour, the history of the city could be seen much more clearly below. The skyscrapers in the east, built during the last few years, the dilapidated blocks of flats dating from the 1950s and 60s, and past them, the ramshackle one or two-storey houses with corrugated iron roofs in the area to the west of the harbour where the Portuguese had first settled, were as distinct as the layers from different geological eras making up a rock mass.

I left the fortress by a different gate, passed under a giant banyan with hundreds of roots and, making my way down a steep hill in the fading light, entered a colonial square paved with mosaics in alternate undulating bands of black and white of a kind often found in Portuguese cities. The first Europeans to "discover" China and master the Chinese techniques of glazing and tile making, the Portuguese had evidently used these accomplishments to decorate, amongst other places, China itself in a style of their own.

One of the buildings with columns and shutters around the square had a sign on it indicating it was the former Senate House of Macao, but its massive wooden double doors were firmly shut. When I saw that, by contrast, the door of the church next door was ajar, a strange instinct to seek shelter indoors at nightfall prompted me to enter.

Three kneeling Chinese were praying separately in the front row, but the pews behind them were empty. Behind the altar, some two or three metres above the floor, was a life-size statue of the Virgin. Her wimple with golden threads in it, her pink-and-white face and the blue gown stretching down to her ankles had been lovingly painted. By each of the sidewalls stood a confessional resembling a gothic phone booth with the crucifix on its pointed roof, and the rest of the space on the walls was taken up with alcoves containing enough further small statues of the Virgin to confirm Protestant bigots in their belief regarding Catholic Mariolatry – Mary as the Queen of Heaven with her crown on her head, Mary as Our Blessed Lady with a halo of stars, Mary as the Mother of God with the baby Jesus in her arms.

For a few moments, I walked around silently amongst these and the votive candles burning on the tables in the corners. Then I stood at the back of the church and looked once again at the three kneeling Chinese praying with closed eyes and clasped fingers to the God the Portuguese had brought. To Mrs Williams' assertion that she didn't understand why men got drunk and turned themselves into beasts, Dr Johnson had replied they were trying to escape the pain of being a man. When I was a student in Chicago, to escape the pain of being young if not of being a man, I had thought of becoming a Catholic myself and, for a while, had even taken instruction from an elderly priest called Father Donovan. Every Tuesday afternoon we would meet at his home smelling of dust and furniture polish, managed by a silent housekeeper, and talk about faith, sin, grace and similar matters on which a young student of literature could in fact produce considerably more interesting ideas than a seventy-year-old man with a limited education. Then our session would be over, and, waiting for a bus in the street outside where Irish housewives went by in misshapen coats in the midst of a grey Chicago winter, I would think of following my conversion by training for the priesthood myself and living with a housekeeper in a home in a poor parish like this one. But, unlike Father Donovan, who believed that God existed in exactly the same way the heavy table and chairs he had brought over from Cork in 1929 existed, I was only after consolation; and since nothing could console a twenty-one-year-old, or, at least, the twenty-one-year-old I was, my enthusiasm for Catholicism had not lasted. Nevertheless, I still remembered the prayers I had learned:

Hail Holy Queen, Mother of Mercy,
our life, our sweetness and our hope
...
after this our exile
show unto us the blessed fruit of thy womb, Jesus
...
pray for us sinners now and at the hour of our death.

I took one last look at the three Chinese who at that moment were perhaps silently uttering those very words, and then walked out. During the short time I had spent in the church, the darkness had thickened outside, and yellow streetlamps had come on around the square. Feeling as if I had turned my back on the light of God, I walked away on the black and white bands of mosaics.

At the bottom of the square there was a road with an occasional car or motor scooter going down it, and on the other side of this stood a two-storey colonial villa with a lit green sign identifying it as "Café Safari". It appeared that the word *seferi*, meaning "on the road", taken to Kenya by Arab traders looking for slaves and ivory, had, after entering Swahili in the form of "safari", made its way here via Portugal's African colonies. Less because I was hungry than because I was tired from all the walking I had done and wanted to sit down, I crossed the road.

Inside the café, green wall lights in keeping with its romantic name were burning, but the walls themselves were slightly dirty, with the plaster cracked and peeling in places, and the empty tables reflecting the early hour created a vague air of lifelessness. I lowered myself into a seat in a corner, briefly studied the menu listing Portuguese dishes, and after waiting for a waitress to emerge from the kitchen, where Chinese voices could be heard in conversation, ordered vegetable soup and spicy chicken.

When I reached the Lisboa after a short walk following my dinner, golden neons were blazing on top of the two main buildings, and on the façade of the annexe there was a large rectangle with red, green and blue lights passing through it while the word "Casino" flashed in the middle. Everything was straight out of Las Vegas.

Going into the casino out of curiosity, I found smoke-filled rooms where, although its being a weekday had kept Hong Kongers away, Chinese from Macao and the mainland were gambling. Looking at male and female croupiers in dinner jackets and bowties, the roulette wheels, the card tables covered in green felt, the devices that automatically threw a pair of dice under a bell jar without allowing anyone to cheat, and the one-armed bandits with their rolling pictures of fruit, I went from room to room, floor to floor. I witnessed a ripple of excitement pass round a whole table from time to time when someone won, and I heard everyone let out their breath in disappointment when the chance to acquire a large sum was lost at the last minute. And when a dispute arose on one occasion, I saw the floor manager called and every single playing card and turquoise-coloured gambling chip on the table counted one by one.

Because I had spent more time on all this than I had realised, it was almost a quarter to ten by the time I went up to my room. Around the circular plaza below, illuminated only dimly by streetlamps and the lights of the hotel, cars were moving slowly like the roulette balls I had just been observing. The fountain in the middle had stopped squirting water, but a plume of liquid resembling a giant feather periodically rose from a bigger fountain in the harbour. The sea was otherwise in darkness, and because they had been built to house offices, the nearby skyscrapers, too, were without lights. It wasn't my usual bedtime, but there was nothing else left for me to do. I switched off my own light and began to undress.

* * *

When I opened my eyes, the weak sun had long risen. Cars were once again going round the plaza, but of the neons and the fountain in the harbour there was no sign. After shaving and taking a shower, I had a cup of tea in my room instead of ordering a full breakfast from room service, and, as it was approaching ten o'clock, I went down and boarded a municipal minibus to go to the very tip of the old colony, the island of Coloane, which was connected to Taipa by a causeway.

Unlike the buses of Hong Kong, fitted with a hi-tech "smartcard" payment system, this vehicle was equipped only with a moneybox next to the driver which had two parallel rods shaped like upside-down "U"s on top of it, with thick square plastic tiles threaded onto these. Seeing that the uppermost tile said "5 ptc", I decided this was the fare on the route and dropping a five-pataca piece in the box, settled in one of the seats covered in pink plastic. The request *Por Favor Não Cuspir* inscribed at a point near the ceiling wasn't as easy to decipher, but assuming that *Cuspir* was an imperative related to the function of a cuspidor, probably meant "Please don't spit".

We began moving and went out on the bridge to Taipa. Because this was built higher in the middle of its two-and-a-half-kilometre span to allow ships to pass under it, our up-and-down progress was not unlike that of a fairground rollercoaster.

On the seafront at Taipa stood a casino even bigger than the one at the Lisboa, probably built as a ploy to attract tourists. Inland, though, there were only old blocks of hotels and shops with faded signs and interiors like the ones I had seen the day before.

The causeway, which we reached after letting off most of the passengers within a few stops, was broad enough to give the impression that Taipa and Coloane were part of the same landmass. As if determined to bolster this sense of continuity, giant pig, monkey, horse and tiger-shaped figures representing signs of the Chinese zodiac stood on the green strip in the middle, keeping up the illusion that we were in a fairground.

On the Coloane side, the driver stopped the minibus next to a queue of lorries waiting to cross the bridge connecting the island to mainland China. But the single passenger left on board apart from me made no move to get out to walk to the People's Republic, and nor did anyone coming over from the other side of the water join us.

When we were eventually underway again, we began by dropping the last passenger off at a stop serving a handful of small houses. Following a road with sharp bends, we then climbed a low hill before coming down the other side and entering a village by the sea. On the edge of a small square, the driver pulled up beside a plastic bottle the size of a man placed on a pavement to advertise Fanta, and, in a tone that indicated this was the final stop, said, "Coloane". Not knowing the Chinese for "Thank you", I said "*Obrigado*" in Portuguese as I stepped out, and then reflected that, in this strange world, this man, too, might be more fluent in Portuguese than he was in Chinese.

Amidst the neglected flowerbeds in the middle of the square was a fountain with the carved figure of an angel as a centrepiece, but it was empty and black with dirt. In front of a greengrocer's on the ground floor of one of the two-storey houses nearby, a woman was sweeping the pavement, while a two- or three-year-old child sat a short distance away, playing by itself. It was as if, after the back streets of Lisbon, I had now arrived in a forgotten village in the heart of Portugal.

As I was gazing at the fish drying on a frame in front of a row of huts just off the square, a man went by on a bicycle and turned into a dusty street. For a while I looked at the red lightbulbs burning inside a small temple with an open front. Then I walked in the other direction, passed a line of young banyans which had just started the process of root generation they would continue with all their lives, and reached a stone monument facing the sea. The inscription on it said it was erected in memory of those killed here while fighting pirates on 12 and 13 June 1910. As there were still pirates in the South China Sea, and they would occasionally hijack a giant tanker and, after killing the crew, sell first the oil and then the ship itself at some port or other, it wasn't surprising that such a fight had taken place in 1910.

Some twenty to thirty metres past the monument, a cat was lapping up water from a brimming plastic bowl in the garden of a house. On the other side of the low wall by the sea, two men, taking advantage of the tide being out, were collecting clams amongst the muddy rocks. Across the channel separating Coloane from the mainland, the nondescript white buildings of China, widely expected to become the superpower of the twenty-first century, looked incredibly near; but I didn't have a visa to set foot amongst them even for a second. Deciding to go back, I began walking towards the bus stop with the giant Fanta bottle.

* * *

After going for a walk to take a last look at Macao, I was only just able to catch the four-o'clock sailing of the jetfoil. As it was Friday, soon the sailings from Hong Kong would be packed with gamblers, but, in the opposite direction, they were once again nearly empty. Despite this, as though determined to keep all the foreigners together, the company officials had placed me next to a tall man approaching sixty, in grey trousers, a navy-blue blazer and a striped tie in the front row of the First Class section.

As soon as we were underway, "Were you in Macao just for a break?" asked my neighbour.

"Yes," I replied.

"Me, too. It's a good place to escape to when Hong Kong gets a bit too much."

Although he had an accent that said, "I've been to Eton, followed by Balliol", there was something about him that wasn't altogether English.

"I am sorry," he said as though he had guessed what I was thinking. "I didn't introduce myself: I am Sergei Andreyevich."

"And I am Savkar Altinel". And we asked simultaneously: "Where are you from?"

"My father's family fled from the Russian Revolution to Shanghai because it was an open city back then and anyone could settle there," he explained. "Their cook Dmitri went with them, so they decided to open a Russian restaurant, but couldn't make a go of it. The chocolate factory they then set up – again thanks to Dmitri – was more successful. My father eventually got married to the daughter of another Russian family in the city, and I was born there in 1944. I don't remember anything of Shanghai, though. When I was old enough to be aware of my surroundings, we were in Hong Kong, this time as refugees from the Chinese Revolution; my father was in the process of re-establishing his chocolate business and I was learning Cantonese from my Chinese ayah."

"So you grew up in Hong Kong?"

"I attended the British School on Victoria Peak for six years before being packed off to school in England. In those days the journey from Hong Kong took three days even if one flew. A Chinese boy named Lee was travelling with me. We spent the first night in Bombay and the second in Beirut. When we landed in London I remember Lee looking at the English porters and saying, 'I thought only the Chinese did such jobs'. Then he went to his school and I went to mine."

"Was that Eton or Harrow?"

He laughed. "Nothing so grand, just Winchester. At school I learnt to eat English food, cope with the cold and be addressed by my surname as 'Chubakov'. Then I read history at Oxford for three years, returned to Hong Kong, married a Chinese girl and took over my father's factory. I was a chocolate manufacturer until two years ago when my wife, who hadn't had a day's illness in her life, suddenly fell down and died one morning. After that I sold my company, so I am retired now."

Clearly, another thing he had learnt in the course of his schooling amongst the English upper classes was talking of the tragedies in his life with a stoical indifference. "And…" I began.

"I think I know what you are going to ask. Ever since the colony was handed over I have been a citizen of the Hong Kong Special Administrative Region of China. After my family spent all their lives running away from the communists, one of the last communist countries in the world has managed to claim me for its own."

"Have you thought of acquiring British nationality and moving to England? It shouldn't be too difficult for someone in your position."

He looked genuinely surprised. "What would I want to live in England for? I've spent most of my life in China, and, yes, I am Chinese. More specifically, I am a Hong Konger. I always end up missing Hong Kong even when I go to Macao for a few days like this."

He then asked me one or two questions about myself, and I told him as much about my background and life as I wished to reveal. By the time I finished talking, we were entering Hong Kong harbour and advertising signs were already glowing against the grey sky on top of some of the skyscrapers.

As we were docking, Sergei Andreyevich stood up and said, "If my wife were alive, I'd have asked you to dinner, but entertaining isn't easy when one's on one's own", before disembarking and walking towards the immigration channel reserved for Hong Kong citizens. Staring at his back, I was struck by the thought that he reminded me of someone, but I couldn't work out whom.

After getting my own passport stamped, I walked out of the terminal, which resembled a shopping centre with its rows of retail outlets. In the road, cars rumbled past, their noise added to by the double-decker trams creaking to a stop to take on or drop off passengers, and the footsteps of those leaving the office buildings on either side.

By exchanging Macao for Hong Kong, where I would be spending two more nights, I had in a sense, moved from the south to the north, from Portugal to Britain, from the provinces to the metropolis. But instead of being elated as a result, I felt strangely subdued. Almost letting myself be swept along by the evening crowd, I reached the plaza in front of the giant skyscraper housing the headquarters of the Hong Kong and Shanghai Bank, and made my way through the subway to the Star Ferry quay to go to my hotel.

I had discovered on previous crossings that just as the green-and-white ferries were symmetrical in construction to enable them to travel back and forth between the two shores without having to manoeuvre, each row of seats on board had a single backrest that could be pushed forward or back so that the seating always faced the direction of travel. As soon as I stepped on to the open upper deck, I made this necessary adjustment to an empty row like a native Hong Konger, before sitting down and proceeding to become engrossed in the harbour view in a way no native Hong Konger would have done.

The usual Indian tailors, descendants of labourers the British had settled in the colony, were waiting in the square behind the quay on the other side. But, ignoring their offers to make me a suit overnight if I accompanied them to their premises to be measured, I turned into Nathan Road.

This thoroughfare, where here and there neons glowed, was also crowded, but no one now went in or out of Kowloon Park, in the mornings full of Chinese doing *tai chi* exercises. As I walked along the wall of the park, that strange mechanism which suddenly allows something we have been trying to remember for hours to rise to the surface of our mind made me realise that the person Sergei Andreyevich reminded me of was Father Donovan, almost certainly long dead by now. There was no physical resemblance between them, but they were both people who led full lives within a confined area with the few bits and pieces that had been dealt out to them. They were like banyans constantly extending and fortifying their roots while I, purposeless and adrift, was still in travel's shabby Café Safari whose plaster had begun to crack. Raising my eyes at the sky, which would soon be darkening, I muttered, "This is our exile; pray for us sinners", but I couldn't be certain my words were sincere. It felt like it was growing cold again. I zipped up my jacket and walked on, looking at the neons, the passers-by, and the traffic.

THE GWANGHWAMUN INTERSECTION

I watched Seoul grow smaller below as, swaying gently, the red-and-white cable car rose into the air. The skyscrapers, bunched together against a backdrop of mountains, some already with snow on top despite it being only September, were reminiscent of Denver or Salt Lake City. Then the images and the Hangul characters on the video hoardings advertising everything from jeans to chocolate became impossible to make out, buildings shrank, cars on roads turned into lines of beads: under the grey sky everything assumed the lifeless appearance of an architectural model.

I wasn't sure why I was here. Like most people living in England, I had some vague ideas about Korea. I knew it was "developed" enough to compete with Japan as an exporter of consumer goods to Europe. My computer and fax machine were Korean-made. I was also used to seeing Hyundai and Daewoo cars in the streets and lumbering yellow Samsung bulldozers and diggers on construction sites. While I had assumed that the businessmen buying and selling these must travel to Korea, however, I had never heard of anyone doing so for pleasure. Then I had read in a guidebook that one of the sights of Seoul was the Gwanghwamun Intersection because, of all the junctions in the city, this was the only one where each of the roads that came together had a different name, and it had occurred to me that it might be strangely liberating to be somewhere featureless enough for such a fact to stand out.

After a long journey that idea now seemed less persuasive. I had arrived in Seoul jet-lagged at eleven in the morning, found a hotel slightly away from the city centre and, after sleeping for several hours, gone out to explore. Despite it being a Sunday, the shops were open and the pavements were crowded. There wasn't a single Westerner in sight, and the entire city smelt of cooking fat as though a giant pot of stew was simmering somewhere. Joining the throngs spending the overcast but warm and humid afternoon shopping, I had walked in and out of gleaming multi-storey outlets and shopping centres different from their European and American counterparts only in being brand new and spotlessly clean, used the escalators and gazed at the familiar products of Givenchy, Versace and Dolce Gabbana. To cross the streets one had to use subways which were in fact arcades lined with further shops, and as the subways seemed to interconnect and extend for miles they gave the impression that, as well as the part of it that could be seen overground, the entire city had a giant basement.

In the end, all these shops, subways, and policemen standing with their long truncheons and transparent plastic shields in front of a police bus parked here and there on a corner had become oppressive and I had begun to feel that a featureless place was more exhausting than liberating. When I had spotted the cable car climbing towards the dark green silhouette of tree-covered Namsan Hill, I had immediately made in that direction.

The skyscrapers below continued to grow smaller. As we ascended, the cable car coming down from the hill went swaying past with Asian faces at the windows. From the windows of our own cabin, where I was one of a handful of passengers without a seat, holding on to straps hanging from the ceiling, I could now see more clearly the leaves of the oaks and beeches on the slope. With a gentle bump we went over one of the outstretched arms of a pylon, climbed a little further and entered the concrete mouth of the terminus waiting for us.

The uniformed young woman who had accompanied us on our journey as though we were in a vehicle that needed to be driven opened the door and, standing on the landing outside, began bowing to each passenger as they left. I bowed back slightly at her, walked out of the station, which wasn't quite at the peak of the hill, and started climbing up the steps leading to the top. The Seoul Tower, indistinguishable (apart from being "the third highest tower in the world") from its ultramodern siblings to be found in other cities of the Far East, rose on top of Namsan. Just as I had not climbed the tower I had seen in Kuala Lumpur two years earlier, I had no intention of climbing this tower either, but I was intrigued to hear loud music as I was approaching the top of the steps. Reaching a piece of level ground surrounded by trees after negotiating the last steep step, I walked towards the sound.

A short distance away stood a hexagonal gazebo with a roof with curved edges like that of a pagoda. In front of this structure, the first example of traditional Korean architecture I had come across since setting foot in the country, what could only be described as a "wall" had been built out of mauve flowers and a stage had been constructed in front of that. As music blared from loudspeakers hidden behind the wall of flowers, two men wearing floppy red caps and purple robes that came down to their ankles were performing a dance which involved a great deal of leaping amongst the life-size figures of cows and pigs on the stage and the occasional tossing at the audience of something the men fished out of their pockets in handfuls.

Hanging overhead from wires attached to the upper branches of the trees on either side were signs in Korean, coloured balloons and small plastic flags of countries, including Turkey, which had taken part in the Korean War half a century earlier; everything was trembling slightly, seemingly as much because of the music as because of the faint breeze on top of the hill. For a while I watched the mysterious performance, too loud to be a religious ceremony and too elaborate to be a folk dance, before walking towards the tower at the other end of the clearing and looking down the back slope of Namsan.

Beyond the steel bridges spanning the lead-coloured Han River, the rest of the city of eleven-and-a-half million souls stretched out in an enormous grey-and-white mass that was unaware of the strange ritual going on above it. On this side, the mass consisted not of skyscrapers but fifteen or twenty-storey apartment blocks interspersed with the odd shorter building. But because there was no sign of life other than a small vessel trailing a barely perceptible wake as it moved upstream, it all once again looked as lifeless as an architectural model.

Following the edge of the clearing, I once again passed under the small plastic flags representing the United Nations, the US, Great Britain, Australia, New Zealand, Canada, Turkey and Greece, turned my back on the stage where the two men were still leaping about, and began walking down the hill. Because it was getting dark, the streetlamps by the narrow asphalt path had come on, and before I had got halfway down the slope, lights also appeared here and there in the skyscrapers, video hoardings came alive and got down to displaying advertisements, and coloured lights resembling those in an amusement park started to blink on and off along the edges of buildings housing stores. Because of this "commercial" light emanating from the city, the sky was now a radiant dome. No longer did the mountains in the background look like the Rockies or Seoul look like an American city.

I could only be in the East, which romantic Westerners imagine to be "mysterious and mystical" but which only seems to pursue concrete and sensible ends like making money and eating.

At the bottom of the path I found myself on a road leading downhill back into the city. Three police buses were parked along the kerb. In front of one of these a group of policemen stood in two neat rows facing one another, smoking in unison as though they were performing a training exercise. Another row of policemen, meanwhile, were sitting on their helmets which they had taken off and placed on the ground to serve as a stool. Each of the buses had a mascot depicted on it in the shape of a flat-nosed dog in police uniform resembling a cartoon character.

A little further on, the iron-barred gates of a courtyard surrounded on three sides by a tall building were shut. Outside, under a brass plate which said "Bank of Korea" in English below an inscription in Hangul characters, there was a U-shaped barricade made of sandbags. Because South Korea was still officially at war with the North, which it simultaneously wanted to reunite with, this was obviously to be used as a machine gun emplacement if the need ever arose. (From the same guidebook which had told me about the Gwanghwamun Intersection I had also learned that there were monthly air raid drills in Seoul, with the sound of the sirens being met by the traffic instantly coming to a halt and everyone temporarily abandoning their vehicle to run for cover.)

Walking along this better-lit road, which the war had not yet reached, I passed the calculators and CD players displayed in the illuminated windows of a long line of shops selling electronic goods. I then turned into a side street and entered the sprawling maze of Nandaemun Market.

The stalls that ran down the middle of the narrow streets lined with small shops on both sides were piled high with fake versions of the clothes and training shoes on offer at the big shopping centres. I then began seeing hand-woven baskets, bowls, crockery and toys. The market leapt from street to street, twisted in and out of tiny alleys, left the middle of the road to invade the pavements as well, going on and on as though it would never end.

Although I was the only foreigner around, nobody pestered me to buy anything. Even when I stood for a long time at a stall selling educational aids and examined, from several angles, a small globe on which the names of the continents written in Korean were accompanied by drawings on the oceans of sailing ships resembling the galleons used by the early European explorers, I was left alone.

As I walked along, from time to time I saw a food stall serving a few customers seated on low stools. In the glare of naked light bulbs, lumps of meat and prawns slowly roasted on skewers; mushrooms and mussels boiled in giant pots; bass and turtles and the first live starfish I had seen in my life swam in the green waters of aquariums as they waited to be killed and eaten.

It was eight o'clock by the time I walked out of the market. With the falling of darkness, the smell of cooking fat in the air seemed to have intensified. Finding my way by road signs, I walked along pavements lined with plane trees that gave a curiously ancient air to this city where nearly everything in fact dated from after the Korean War. Once I had left the centre behind, few people were about in the streets, and the neighbourhood of my hotel looked particularly deserted. Spotting a single-storey building next door to a petrol station, with a purple neon sign in the shape of a dragon, under which the words *Chinese Restaurant* flashed in English, I went in.

On the left were a pair of cubicles in which two Korean families were seated cross-legged on small mats, silently eating. But, although it was still quite early, the main dining area, furnished not with mats but tables and chairs, was empty. A waitress in heavy make-up was running a wet mop over the polished wooden floor while two of her colleagues wearing yellow rubber gloves could be seen washing dishes through the open door of the kitchen.

A man in a white apron, whom I took to be the owner, materialised, holding a long red menu, motioned to me to sit down and said, "English?"

"Yes, please," I replied, taking the menu and choosing crab with rice from amongst the dishes whose names were typed in English on a yellowing sheet of paper. As I was to learn over the next few days to be customary in Korea, a waitress first brought me a glass of water and a small dish of spicy kimchi pickles. This was followed by a bowl of virtually clear soup with a few pieces of vegetables floating in it, and finally my order arrived.

Coming up to me again after I had taken a bite or two of this, the owner said, "Everything good?"

"Everything's fine."

"Kimchi enough?"

"More than."

Nodding with the satisfied air of a man who had done his duty, he seated himself at one of the empty tables and, leaving me to my chopsticks and his staff to their cleaning tasks, began to watch a taekwondo contest on the television set occupying a shelf mounted three quarters of the way up the wall.

When I finished my meal, I interrupted his viewing to pay the bill of 9,000 won and made my way through the adjacent petrol station to a small grocer's that was still open. I bought a bottle of water from the old woman behind the narrow counter, bowed in response to her bowed thanks, and walked along the half-dark street, swinging my plastic bag.

In the window of a pet shop immediately next to my hotel, two puppies were fast asleep, huddled together. For a moment I looked at their silent breathing before going up to my room and finding a local TV channel broadcasting to the American forces in Korea on which I watched obscure old films interspersed with breaks for words of guidance ("Don't forget that Koreans are our friends", "You are here as representatives of your country", "A soldier always takes care of his rifle") until the early hours.

* * *

When I opened my eyes to the rising sound of traffic, the day outside was once again overcast although clearly destined eventually to become uncomfortably warm. The grey buildings across the road, each with a large yellow plastic water tank on the roof, looked as if they were already feeling the heat a little.

I got dressed and went out, and, picking up an English-language *Korea Herald* at a newsstand, began walking without any idea of where I was going. A group of schoolchildren went by with their satchels on their backs; two girls in high heels deftly ran to catch an orange-and-white city bus pulling in at a stop a hundred yards away; above the pavement an advertisement, grown faint in daylight, still flickered on a video hoarding.

In a supermarket there were people eating at a breakfast counter. I went in, picked up a cake and a paper cup with a teabag in it, got hot water from a shiny steel cistern placed on a small table and moving over to the counter, opened my paper.

The Ministry for Unification was prepared to lend North Korea one hundred million dollars to help this "starving communist land". The loan, made at a token rate of interest of one percent, would strengthen the ties between the two countries. The United States was also holding disarmament talks with the North but was worried by President Kim Jong-il's intransigent attitude. Meanwhile Seoul, where a series of new restaurants and entertainment venues had opened recently, continued to be one of Asia's leading cities.

I threw the paper, which also had a section where some of the news items were translated into Korean for the benefit of those learning English, in the bin and walked out. The underground station a little further down the road was filled with young managers on their way to work in dark suits despite the threat of a hot day. I joined them in their crowded train and was soon amongst the skyscrapers at the city centre, once again breathing in Seoul's warm air smelling of cooking fat.

Hawkers were displaying their wares on the pavement outside Lotte, the largest and most impressive of the department stores I had seen the previous day. A man, who had managed to carve out quite a large space for himself and the tennis balls he was selling amongst those offering other goods such as socks and lighters, kept whacking with a racket at a ball he had attached with a long piece of elastic to a weight on the ground. For a few seconds I stood there, watching him, before walking round the corner and going in through the revolving doors of the Lotte Hotel.

Apart from uniformed staff soundlessly moving this way and that on thick strips of red carpet, there was no one about in the lobby which was massive enough to remain a little dim despite the giant cluster of light bulbs suspended from the ceiling for which the word "chandelier" was hardly adequate. On the wall behind the long reception counter there was, not a row of clocks showing the time in a few selected cities, as there would have been at a lesser hotel, but a large electronic map on which digital figures showed the time in every single country in the world. In Turkey it was three o'clock in the morning, in England it was one, and in Chicago it was still six in the evening on the previous day. It was as if everything that had contributed to my formation had vanished into the past and the dark, leaving me alone in this alien city with no option but to keep walking and looking around.

A little beyond Reception, in a dining room with an open front facing the lobby, a few guests were sipping their morning coffee from china cups at tables covered in white linen. Behind the huge pane of glass that made up the opposite wall an artificial waterfall tumbled between real rocks and vines. There seemed to be nothing other than a few gift shops further ahead. I made my way back to the revolving doors and walked out of the hotel.

Because most of those in the city were at work, Seoul was less crowded today. As the wide roads largely prevented traffic sounds from echoing off the buildings, the noise level wasn't high either. The flood consisting of orange-and-white buses, courier motorcycles and Hyundais, most of which seemed to be black, white or grey, flowed past with a muted rumble. It was as if I was watching everything on a television set with the sound turned down.

A big airline office was followed by a number of hotels that were clearly expensive, even though, equally clearly, they weren't in the same league as the Lotte. Then, amidst the façades of the skyscrapers filled with row after row of windows ahead, I finally saw the spot I had travelled thousands of kilometres to reach: the Gwanghwamun Intersection.

On a high rectangular stone plinth at the centre of it stood a black statue of Admiral Yi Sun-sin in a long suit of armour of thick leather and a matching helmet that came down to his shoulders. His right hand was wrapped in a defiant manner around the hilt of his long sword whose tip rested on the ground, and his other hand was placed on his hip. Yi was perhaps the greatest national hero of the Koreans, who, prior to beginning to fight one another, had spent their history fighting the Japanese. In the last years of the sixteenth century he had had a small fleet of conventional wooden vessels covered in iron plating and, using these first armoured craft in history, which he referred to as "turtle ships", inflicted a heavy defeat on the Japanese navy, saving Korea from invasion.

The Admiral's face was turned towards one of his old haunts, the Gyeongbokgung Palace at the end of the broadest of the roads coming together at the intersection which were famous for each of them having a different name. I wasn't particularly interested in the Palace, home of the Chosun dynasty which had ruled Korea for three hundred years after Yi's death until the Japanese finally managed to seize the country in 1910. But the way the structure appeared to be directly at the foot of the mountains I had seen from the cable car the day before was attractive. Without much hesitation I began walking in that direction.

Once again, groups of policemen equipped with truncheons and shields waited here and there along the road. As North Korea was only forty kilometres away and there had been occasions in the past when a special team stole across the border to assassinate a Southern politician or plant a bomb in a public place, perhaps they were right to wait. But it looked as if I had missed the monthly air raid drill: I didn't get to see everyone run to take cover in underground stations and subways as the sirens began to wail.

At one point I had to wait at a corner as a black limousine whose interior was invisible behind its tinted windows entered the American Embassy compound equally invisible behind its high walls. When I could start walking again and approached the Palace, which stood on the other side of the T-junction the road ended in, I saw signs of recent restoration work on the not altogether impressive structure.

The humped tiles covering the oriental roof with curved edges were new, and the carved eaves had been fashioned out of concrete, a material probably not known in the early days of the Chosun dynasty, and they were still waiting to be painted.

To add to the picture, there was scaffolding here and there around the big stone courtyard I found myself in after crossing the road and going in through the arched gate. In a corner a man was mixing cement, and the sound of hammering came from somewhere. But there was something desultory and half-hearted about these efforts, as though, rather than use its energies to preserve the past, Seoul would have preferred to add to the skyscrapers that looked in over the wall surrounding the palace grounds.

A handful of visitors reduced to insignificance by the immensity of the courtyard were busy photographing one another in front of the buildings, which couldn't be entered because of the ongoing repairs. A couple with young children were trying to cope with the discomfort of having nothing to offer to the pigeons milling about their feet, looking for food. An Indian with his hands in his pockets, the first foreigner I had come across in Korea, was gazing at the grey mountain peaks with patches of snow on them in the distance, as if, like me, he, too, had decided they were the only sight really worth seeing here.

As I walked out of the palace, I turned round to take another look at those peaks myself. I knew from evenings in Chicago long ago when I had watched Hawkeye Pierce and his fellow-surgeons shivering and hugging themselves in their tents in *M*A*S*H* that winters were bitter in Korea, and just as earlier on, I had imagined a sudden air raid, I now tried to imagine the snow coming down from the mountains into the city and covering the streets, the exhaust fumes of vehicles becoming cloudy and visible in the cold, and everything being transformed into a film which had not only had its sound turned down but was also in black and white. Seoul might have been more interesting under such conditions, but of course winter was still months away; the day had begun to get warmer as I had expected, and as well as smelling faintly of cooking fat and emitting a faint rumble of traffic, the city continued to be faintly oppressive. Unable to think of anything else to do, I walked for another half hour till I reached Tapgol Park.

At the entrance, a hawker was selling small Korean flags from a tray slung round his neck, and immediately inside the gates a stone statue of Son Byong-hi continued the theme of patriotism. Just as Admiral Yi's victory over the Japanese navy had enabled the Chosun dynasty to last – albeit with some difficulty – for another three hundred years, Son had challenged Japanese domination in the twentieth century and by reading out a Declaration of Independence with a group of like-minded individuals in this park had, in a sense, laid the foundations of modern Korea.

Behind the statue was an asphalt path that seemed to go all the way round the park. Under the plane trees along this, old men dressed in white sat talking in small groups on the few benches that were available or directly on the grass. It was obvious that, like me, they, too, were idle and had come here because there was little else to do in the vast city. Not content that their entire lives had vanished, they were waiting for another day to pass. One or two of them gazed at me briefly as I went by before turning back to his companions.

The path led to a set of bronze reliefs at the other end of the park depicting the savagery with which the Japanese, destined to stay in the country until 1945 despite Son's efforts, had suppressed the independence movement. I looked at panels showing prisoners being shot, patriots being sent into exile and women weeping as their menfolk were taken away;

then, briefly attracting the attention of other white-clad old men sitting in the shade of other plane trees, I followed the rest of the path until it took me back to the gates.

The sun on the pavements outside indicated noon had come. I wasn't hungry, but to sit and think about what I would do next, I walked into a nearby cafeteria and decided over lunch to go and take a look at the Han River.

There were apartment blocks along the opposite side of the road I reached after a long journey on the underground. When I turned my back on them, though, I could see that on my side a set of steps descended to a broad strip of grass and beyond that was the river, spanned by bridges, only one or two of which had vehicles on them. On the opposite bank there were once again apartment blocks and tree-covered hills. There appeared to be even less to see in this part of the city than in the part between Namsan and the mountains to the north.

People were sitting under white triangular canvas shades held up by metal poles on the strip of grass, and a few walkers were strolling by the water, the heavy black umbrellas they held up doing duty as parasols against the now burning sun. Ignoring the rays trying to smash through my skull, I went down the steps myself and, after walking for a minute or two, spotted a double-decker tour boat at a long concrete jetty ahead.

Although the jetty looked deserted from a distance, a small booking office was open. It was clear that the woman inside had no English, but the fact that a large metal sign, shaped like a clock and equipped with hands that could be set manually to the desired time, pointed to three o'clock indicated that the next river tour would be starting then. I bought a ticket and began to wait.

In time I was joined by ten or fifteen other passengers. Then there was a movement behind us, and two crew members made their way past the queue and opened the hatchway in the side of the vessel. When everyone began writing something on the back of their ticket, I at first couldn't work out what they were doing, but, seeing they were consulting photographed ID cards they had taken out of their pocket, realised they were writing down their name and card number. It wasn't clear whether the aim was to prove they weren't North Korean agents or ensure their body could be identified if the boat sank and they drowned in the waters of the Han. But following suit and scribbling my own name on the back, I handed my ticket to the crew member at the hatchway, climbed to the upper deck and sat in one of the seats out in the open.

After all this, the tour itself didn't last very long. Slowly we pulled away from the jetty to the middle of the river and, passing under the arches of one bridge after another, made our way upstream between the apartment blocks on either side with their windows glinting like mirrors. Because the Han reached the sea in North Korea and therefore could not be used for transport despite being wide and deep enough to be navigable, the only other vessel to be seen was a brand-new speedboat moored at a small landing on the left bank. It took us about twenty-five minutes to come abeam of Namsan Hill standing under the sun with the Seoul Tower on top of it. We then executed an easy manoeuvre in the empty waters to reverse our direction, passed under the same bridges one by one and reached the jetty we had departed from. The cruise was over.

Walking past a crew member bowing to the departing passengers as usual, I stepped ashore. A group of Koreans who had got out of the boat before me were still turning round from time to time to cast a longing glance back as if unable to tear themselves away from the marvels they had seen. Leaving them behind, I went up the steps leading to the road behind the jetty, stubbornly walked along the bank for more than an hour and returned via back streets to my starting point. But I saw nothing other than apartment blocks like the ones I had seen from the tour boat and some smaller buildings identical, down to their rooftop water tank made of yellow plastic, to the buildings I had seen that morning from the window of my hotel room.

By the time I got back to the city centre it had grown dark and video hoardings had once more come alive. The streets were full of young people looking for fun, some of whom had dyed their hair an artificial colour such as orange or lime green. In front of the Lotte department store, the same man was hitting the same tennis ball with the same racket in a way that suggested that was what he had spent the whole day doing. There was something disheartening in the thought that he would still be here, hitting with the same *thwack thwack thwack* long after I had left Korea.

Turning into a side street, I came across a local preacher continuing the work begun by the American missionaries who had managed to convert a quarter of Koreans to Protestantism in the nineteenth century. He had a large crucifix round his neck and was speaking in a monotonous tone into a microphone he had connected to a portable amplifier. A group of young men who might have been some of the managers I had seen on the underground that morning were approaching from the other direction, but they had now loosened their ties and slung their jackets over their arms. It looked as if they had stopped at a bar and had a few drinks after work: their gait was a little unsteady and they were casting furtive looks at the slender-waisted Korean girls going by. It was as if the street preacher was addressing them. Perhaps the word *nemoye*, which he kept repeating, meant “repent”. But it didn’t seem as if he would get any sinners to change their ways in the near future. Leaving him to his sermon, I walked away, wondering how to spend my evening.

★ ★ ★

I wandered about Seoul for another day and a half, discovering a handful of striking features under the featureless surface of the city. I saw the pairs of spectacles attached by a length of chain to bank counters for the benefit of short-sighted customers wishing to sign a cheque or withdraw money, the fortune tellers reading palms in tiny tents pitched on crowded pavements, the policemen directing traffic after dark with illuminated batons like lightsabres out of *Star Wars*. I figured out that *puk* and *nam*, which occurred frequently in place names, stood for "north" and "south", and I learnt to say not "Thank you" but *Kamsahamnida* when I bowed to express my gratitude. Then I couldn't take it any more, so I fled.

Nobody other than me had got off at Namyong, one of the stations along the stretch where Line 1 of the Underground emerged on the surface to become an ordinary suburban railway. I walked along a road almost deserted in the middle of the afternoon, turned right and realised I had reached the Yongsan Base of the United States Army when I saw the policemen standing in front of a long stone wall a short distance ahead.

What I was after was not the base itself but the USO centre next door. The base was strictly for those serving under the Stars and Stripes, while I knew that the United Services Organizations, set up during the Second World War to meet the rest and recuperation needs of members of the American armed forces, also catered to civilians of all nationalities.

The Seoul branch of the USO was a single-storey structure. Its whitewashed walls sported a number of amateurishly drawn pictures devoted to all-American subjects such as the Statue of Liberty, a family walking their dog and a group of children playing basketball, and above these, large capitals spelt out the claim "WHEN YOU ARE AWAY FROM HOME, WE BRING HOME TO YOU".

To me America was not home but just a memory. And it couldn't be said to be a happy memory either; I had convinced myself I didn't like the country and for four years had felt little except impatience and frustration. All that, though, now appeared to me as just youth, and when I looked back I saw not so much youth's perpetual turmoil as its boundless energy. This was why when I had got bored in Seoul I had been driven here by a momentary need to seek contact with the past. I pushed the door and went in.

Photographs of USO staff looked from one wall of a short corridor and facing them on the other wall was a cork board with notices pinned to it. Those wishing to spend Thanksgiving in Tokyo had to inform Mrs Brown who was organising the charter flight; Korean lessons had been moved from Friday to Wednesday evenings; there would be an Orientation tour of Seoul at the end of the month for new arrivals.

One or two people were working in the glass-fronted offices along one side of the lounge the corridor led to, but there was no one in the sitting area itself. In one corner a half-eaten cake with the inscription "Good Luck to Tom in His New Job" stood on a table with a stack of paper plates next to it. In the opposite corner a television set with a screen at least four times the normal size was showing what appeared to be an episode of a serial about a rich but unhappy family. At the bottom of the lounge was another short corridor and at the bottom of that a neon sign that said "Canteen".

When I went through the door under the sign I found blue Formica-topped tables sandwiched between long seats upholstered in red plastic. It was clear that the intention was for the colour scheme to recall the American flag and the general atmosphere to recall a diner in the middle of America where they had been grilling hamburgers and pouring Coca-Cola into glasses for decades. The fans on the ceiling and the jukebox by the wall opposite the entrance completed the décor.

Because lunchtime had passed, the tables were empty, but a young American was sitting at the till and there was a Korean woman behind the self-service counter. As I had used to years earlier, I got myself a steak sandwich, a slice of apple pie and an iced tea, and ate my meal without trying to convince myself that nothing had changed.

When I walked out of the canteen, two black men were seated in front of the TV, watching the row a ridiculously well-dressed woman was having with a ridiculously handsome man in a room full of expensive furniture on the screen.

The black man who was nearer to me looked up and said, "Haven't seen you before; have you just come from the States?" He might not have been from the South, but, like a substantial number of blacks, he spoke in a version of the southern accent acquired in the cotton fields by his ancestors.

"I'm not American."

"Are you one of those Brits who teach English?

"No."

"What are you doing in Seoul then?"

"Good question: what's there to do in Seoul?"

"Don't ask us," said the other black man, laughing without taking his eyes off the TV. "The Army said come, so we came."

Envious of them for being part of a bigger whole despite everything, I made for the door. As I was going out, the woman on the screen behind me hissed: "That's right, just walk away: what else have you ever done?"

I stood still for a second on the pavement, then I made my decision. The only fixed point in my life apart from my youth was my childhood although it was not as important to me.

The leather-bound collections of old news magazines on my parents' bookshelves I had begun to pore over as soon as I had learnt to read at the end of the 1950s were still vivid in my mind with their black-and-white photographs and the captions accompanying them: "Turks by the Yellow Sea", "Our heroes in Korea", "Kunuri", "Panmunjom". I could soon be amongst all these.

The "War Memorial" in the district of Itaewon was in fact not a war memorial but a museum in vast grounds with an impressive collection of military aircraft parked along one side. The poles by the broad path climbing at a gentle angle to the main building once again had the flags of the nations that had participated in the Korean War flying from them. These, though, were more serious-looking and more in keeping with historical facts than the small plastic flags I had seen on my first day in the city. The flag of Canada, next to the Turkish flag, was not the country's present one with a maple leaf on it but the red flag with a Union Jack in one corner it used at the time of the war. On inspection, even the Turkish flag turned out not to be the Turkish flag but the colours of the Turkish Armed Forces, with initials attesting to this fact in the upper left-hand corner.

Although the ticket I bought at the door for 5,000 won had a picture on it showing soldiers in steel helmets storming a hill, along with the date 25 June 1950, when the Korean War had started, the museum covered not just this but all wars in the history of Korea. But I wasn't particularly interested in these other conflicts: I quickly walked past glass cases containing prehistoric spear heads dug up by archaeologists, some rusting swords and guns, and a model of an old armoured vessel that had to be one of Admiral Yi's turtle ships, and went up to the first floor devoted to the Korean War.

Around the large circular entrance hall, six film screens had been placed that followed the curvature of the walls.

In the old newsreels projected on to these from equipment mounted on the ceiling, the war was still in progress. Soldiers were advancing behind tanks, planes were diving to attack railway lines, warships were bombarding coastal towns.

In the main exhibit area entered through this film room, two men were reading, in low murmurs, the captions in Korean on the large photographs displayed in the cases embedded in the walls. Standing beside them, I looked at the English translations of the same captions. It appeared that, like much else in Korean history, the war had come about because of the country's relations with the Japanese. Having defeated Japan, the Allies had also seized Korea, at that time a Japanese possession, and it had been decided that the Soviet Union would occupy the part to the north and the United States to the south of the 38th Parallel. In 1948, the occupiers had withdrawn, leaving behind them two rival governments, each laying claim to all of Korea, and in 1950 the North Koreans had crossed the 38th Parallel in Soviet-made T-34 tanks to attack the South.

In a large case nearby there were mannequins in the uniforms of Army, Navy and Air Force officers from the North and the South. Because there had been women combatants on both sides, two of the mannequins represented women. An explanatory note indicated, however, that the South had not in fact had armed forces but only a police force at the outbreak of the war, and its stock of armaments had been limited. While the North had had 242 tanks, 2,318 pieces of artillery and 211 aircraft, the South had had no tanks and only 91 pieces of artillery and 22 aircraft.

Next, I saw a large model depicting a group of civilians trying to defend themselves in front of a half-demolished building. The extremely well-made figures, each of them about a metre high, had strips of white fabric with Korean writing on them tied round their heads. A few of them also had large bloodstains on their shirts that showed they were wounded, and one lay dead in the ruins behind. Bending to look at the explanation under the model, I discovered that I had been looking at university students who, having volunteered to join the fighting after the North Koreans reached Seoul within three days, had managed to put up a long resistance in a girls' school on the outskirts of the city. The next case contained the students' military-style peaked caps, identity cards and letters to their families.

Still muttering, the two Koreans had walked away. I could hear other people talking in low voices here and there, but there was only a handful of visitors in the huge room. Hearing my footsteps echoing in the silence, I followed the yellow arrows painted on the floor.

The next stage was the entry of the Americans into the war. After the Northern forces had driven the South Koreans almost to the bottom of the peninsula, General MacArthur had decided that the only solution was a landing at Inchon behind enemy lines. In the detailed model of the landing, red lights representing artillery fire flashed amongst the buildings on the shore, and the attacking warships responded with red flashes of their own.

MacArthur and I seemed to be following one another. Eight years earlier, while travelling in Australia, I had stood on a hilltop in Alice Springs one hot afternoon, thinking about the General arriving in this small, dusty town at the heart of the Outback in a military DC-3 in 1942 after the invading Japanese had forced him to flee from the Philippines. Now, in the midst of another war, we were reunited.

The difference was that in Korea MacArthur had won. He had made his landing and, swiftly retaking Seoul and handing it over to the South Korean president Syngman Rhee, had continued his advance until he captured the Northern capital Pyongyang. The photographs in the cases showed Southern soldiers raising their own flag over Pyongyang Town Hall and Rhee entering the town amidst cheering crowds, with his wire-rimmed spectacles glinting in the sun.

All these triumphs, though, had merely caused the Northerners to turn to the Chinese for assistance, and with the entry of these new belligerents into the war, the South Koreans had, before long, been forced to withdraw to their own territory. A model, once again employing figures about a metre high, showed Chinese troops advancing towards Southern positions, and the note below indicated that they always attacked in waves and, as they approached, kept blowing bugles and banging gongs "to strike terror" into the defenders. I didn't know if puppet making was a traditional Korean craft, but, like the student volunteers, these enemy soldiers, too, were depicted with amazing realism.

The model was followed by a case containing a life-size mannequin in a white winter uniform designed to provide camouflage against the snow. At its feet lay a Chinese flag riddled with bullet holes and a collection of objects found on captured Chinese fighters. A gas mask and a gong were accompanied by a tube of toothpaste, a bar of soap with Chinese characters carved on it, a crumpled packet of cigarettes and a box of "Double Happiness" matches which, for some reason, had their name, and the fact that they were manufactured in Shanghai, written in English. It was strange to think that all these had once belonged to real people who had brushed their teeth, washed their hands, in rare quiet moments lit a cigarette with Double Happiness even, and perhaps were still alive somewhere.

There was little space devoted to the period after the entry of China, when the war had dragged on inconclusively for months, or to the two years of ceasefire talks that had followed. This was clearly because the South did not recognise the treaty finally signed between the United States, China and the North in 1953, and persisted in its claim to all of the country. The model of the Ceasefire Line and the Demilitarised Zone straddling it, both of them still very much in force, was, as usual, highly detailed, but the scale was smaller, as though to minimise the acknowledgement given to the existence of North Korea.

The few exhibits left in the room after this point concerned the documenting and reporting of the war. Next to giant film cameras on tripods were reel-to-reel tape recorders as big as trunks and record players and vinyl discs used for broadcasting propaganda to the enemy. All these old machines and the news magazines from the 1950s accompanying them could have come straight from my childhood forty years ago in another country thousands of miles away.

The museum had surprised me a little. Despite the flags flying from the poles outside, I had come across nothing about most of the foreign nations that had fought in Korea. Although, out of necessity, the Americans were referred to in some measure, the war was presented as something that had essentially occurred between the North, the South, and China. When I followed the yellow arrows up to the next floor, though, I found it was devoted entirely to those who had joined the conflict as the "United Nations Contingent".

Participants in this capacity ranged from Britain and France to a host of countries like Greece, Ethiopia, Colombia, Thailand and South Africa which few would associate with the Korean War. In addition, Italy, Denmark, Sweden, Norway and India, while not contributing military personnel or equipment, had sent medical units. Mannequins in the uniforms of all these countries stood in a giant glass case in the middle of the room, and along the walls there were cases devoted to individual nations. Greek pilots climbing into their jets, Colombians on their way to the front, Turks being served food by Korean women filled old photographs.

When I spotted the flag icons displayed on a computer monitor standing on a squat plinth, I touched the Turkish flag and looked at the information that appeared. The first Turkish forces, consisting of two infantry battalions accompanied by one artillery battalion had disembarked in Korea on 17 October 1950, with Turkey sending a total of 14,936 troops to the country over the course of the war and losing 724 of them in the fighting. The British dead, meanwhile, numbered 1,086 out of the 62,000 personnel deployed.

One of the last exhibits was a model of the United Nations Cemetery where all the foreign dead were buried. The Turkish graves, identifiable by their Crescent-and-Star emblem were immediately at the front, but even so the inscriptions on them were too small to make out. Only the name of Private Şükrü Erdoğan, fallen at the age of twenty-one on 28 November 1950 and lying in a grave even further forward than the rest, was legible.

I walked out of the room and slowly made my way down the empty stairs. The Ceasefire Line and the Demilitarised Zone created after the war might have been dealt with somewhat sketchily inside, but a table by the exit was covered in a variety of colour brochures, each of them with the words "Demilitarised Zone" on it. Leafing through one or two, I discovered they belonged to companies running tours to the ceasefire area to the north of Seoul. I chose one that said, "We can pick you up from your hotel", used the payphone mounted on the wall to dial the number and said to the woman who answered, "I'd like to join tomorrow's tour".

* * *

The next morning a petite girl was waiting for me in the lobby. She was dressed in a grey t-shirt with a grey skirt and trainers, and she had red highlights in her hair. Like her appearance, her manner, too, was more informal than that of most of the Koreans I had met so far. "My name is Moon," she said, smiling and pointing at the ceiling, "like the one in the sky. Did they tell you that you must have your passport with you on this tour?"

I confirmed that they had and we went out together and walked over to a black minibus parked a little distance away that had the inscription "Super Tours" on its side in English. There was no one inside other than a Korean at the wheel. "This is our driver Mr Lee," explained Moon when we had got into our seats. "First we'll pick up two other people, and then we'll go to the Demilitarised Zone. After that, you'll have lunch as part of the tour; it'll probably be three or so before we are back in the city." Quickly saying "Excuse me", she then answered her mobile which had begun ringing just as the minibus was pulling away from the kerb.

The nondescript buildings and orderly traffic of Seoul were going by outside. Even for a city attracting so few foreigners, three people hardly amounted to a large number for a tour. The fact that, for a mere 48,000 won a head we would avail ourselves of the services of Moon and Mr Lee for half a day and have a meal on top of that indicated who still ruled the world. Korea might look more "developed" than many Western countries, but economic superiority clearly lay with Westerners who could easily afford such sums.

Moon had finished her impenetrable conversation in Korean. She switched her mobile off, and, turning back to me, asked, a little flirtatiously: "So are you backpacking around the world then?"

"I am a bit old for that sort of thing; you could say I was *holdalling*."

She laughed. "Are you English or American?"

"Neither. I live in England, but I am Turkish."

"How long have you been in Seoul?"

"This is my fourth day. Tomorrow I go to Busan." The idea had occurred to me as I was speaking. It was a condition of the cheap air ticket that had brought me here via Amsterdam that I stay in Korea for at least a week. If I travelled all the way to the other end of this far-from-large country the next day, I could spend two nights in the southern port of Busan, return to Seoul on Saturday and fly to Amsterdam the next morning.

We had reached the Gwanghwamun Intersection. "Do you know who that is?" Moon said, pointing at the big black statue on its stone plinth.

"Admiral Yi," I told her, "the man who had the Turtle Ships built."

She raised her eyebrows in an exaggerated gesture of admiration. "I can tell you are European; you know everything."

I wasn't sure if, in her eyes, the omniscience she attributed to Europeans distinguished them from Asians or from Americans, a nation she had earlier thought I might belong to. I responded with a vague nod which could mean anything.

Before long, we had left the centre and entered a broad thoroughfare between high-rise apartment blocks and business establishments which looked as if it would soon turn into a road leading out of the city. When we pulled over to the right and stopped, Moon explained that the two people who would be joining us would be arriving in a minibus heading for Seoul with a different tour group. Then, taking advantage of the break in the journey, she asked for my passport and began copying the information in it onto a piece of paper.

As she wrote, she was humming a fast-paced pop tune. It wasn't clear if she wanted to show me how much fun we were going to have together or was already bored with this trip which she must have made many times before. There was something childish about all her actions that made it difficult for me to estimate her age. As she gave my passport back to me, to pass the time, I nodded towards the Hangul lettering on the signs of the businesses and remarked that the Korean alphabet looked as if it might be easier to master than its Chinese or Japanese counterparts. Moon began to explain that, because the characters were both clearer in outline and much fewer in number, they could indeed be learnt more quickly, and, as a result, the country's literacy rate had been very high for years. But the appearance of another minibus bearing the inscription "Super Tours" on the opposite side of the road cut our conversation short.

The newcomers were a somewhat stout young man of medium height who was already balding even though he didn't look as if he was yet thirty, and an Oriental girl. Even before the young man introduced himself as Chuck the minute he stepped into our minibus, I could tell he was American. When the girl then said she was Blossom, I at first thought she was a Hong Kong Chinese who found it convenient to use a Western name in her dealings with Westerners. But the booklet she handed to Moon from the seat behind me where she had positioned herself next to Chuck, was a claret-coloured People's Republic of China passport embossed with golden stars. Not only Korea's granting entry to citizens of her enemy of half a century earlier, but also the fact of the Chinese being allowed to have passports in the first place were signs we were living in a changing world.

"Watch out, she could be a spy!" Chuck said, roaring with laughter at the sight of Moon poring carefully over the pages of Blossom's passport.

"Do I look like a spy?" asked Blossom.

As the question was clearly aimed at Moon and me, I opened my mouth to say no, but it immediately became obvious that, with Chuck around, no one else would get much of a chance to speak. He began by explaining that he was in the US Navy. He was stationed at a base in Japan. Blossom, whom he had known for two years, meanwhile, was a nurse in Singapore. They visited each other whenever they could and, from time to time, went travelling together elsewhere in Asia like this. Chuck loved the Navy. Some years ago, the US had decided to make defence cuts and let many servicemen go, but then it had realised it needed those people to defend its interests. Only recently, they had paid Chuck a bonus of 45,000 dollars to get him to stay in the Navy for another five years.

He then went on to airfares. These were very cheap in Japan. Chuck's ticket to Korea had cost him only 300 dollars, return. The next day he was flying back to Japan, but he'd stay there for only a few hours before flying to Thailand for the four days remaining of his leave. His mother, whom he hadn't seen for three years, wanted Chuck to return to the States, but he first wanted to see the world. He was actually going home for Christmas this year, but once the holidays were over he'd head straight back to Japan.

Talking of Christmas had reminded Chuck of snow. This was the only thing about Japan that he didn't like. Being from Galveston, he wasn't used to hard winters. But he'd arrived at his base in the middle of a blizzard, and, for many winters now, he'd seen nothing but snow. Only last February more than a metre of snow had fallen.

I could see he was so garrulous not because he was American but because he was happy. He was young, he had money, he had found himself a girlfriend, he was travelling. Unable to believe all this was real, he was talking as though he was running to keep up with his rapidly expanding happiness, and, by making jokes all the time he was trying to show Blossom how close they were and to provoke her into running with him.

I couldn't tell him about happiness being at once powerful enough to fill the whole world and light up everything, and fragile enough to be shattered and gone in an instant. Perhaps, when he looked back years later, he would see this moment, when he was riding in a minibus towards the Demilitarised Zone outside Seoul in the company of a strange Turk, still shining brightly amidst the dust of time, and wonder how things could have gone so wrong so soon afterwards.

I leaned forward and began looking out of the window. We were travelling by the Han River which, after leaving Seoul, had turned northwards and was flowing towards North Korea where it would soon reach the sea. Here and there loops of barbed wire and watchtowers stood along the bank, and from time to time I saw a piece of artillery guarded by a pair of soldiers.

"Sometimes Northerners turn up in rubber dinghies and try to land," explained Moon. "That's why we have to have all these." Then, pointing at the green hills beyond a distant bend of the river, she added in a tone designed to shock us, "That's North Korea over there."

On a hillside stood two tall poles with a number of long horizontal metal bars between them, each sporting a row of lightbulbs. "What's that?" I asked.

"A message panel. They can jam our radio and television broadcasts electronically, but they can't prevent us from putting messages on panels like those."

The lightbulbs looked small and harmless under the sun, but I imagined them coming to life after dark and the Hangul characters gliding past like pale ghosts, saying, "Money, security, freedom, we've got it all. In the meantime, you are starving to death. Would you like to borrow a hundred million dollars, or, better still, be united with us?" to the North Korean soldiers waiting in their own watchtowers across the water.

The road had left the bank, and there were now hills on either side. Before long, a row of checkpoints resembling tollbooths appeared ahead. A few other tour vehicles had stopped to be checked. As Mr Lee pulled up at one of the booths, we were approached by a man looking like a plainclothes police officer and two soldiers in camouflage gear who held the automatic weapons slung from their shoulders parallel to the ground in readiness. The plainclothes man slid the door of the minibus open, studied first the information Moon had copied from our passports, then the passports themselves, and finally our faces. Then, without saying anything, he handed our documents back and shut the door. We moved on.

"Phew, that was close," Chuck told Blossom. "They could've got you there." Then he turned to Moon and asked: "Are we in the Demilitarised Zone now?"

"No, but we will be soon."

Beyond the checkpoints, the road had narrowed. We passed between green rice paddies and turned into an even narrower road that spiralled its way up a hill through a wood. Birdsong drifted from the trees.

But these signs of tranquillity were deceptive. Arrow-shaped tin signs painted half red and half white were nailed to small stakes by the side of the road. "The white tips of the arrows indicate the road is safe, but there are mines on the red side," said Moon. Once again, she sounded like a child trying to scare her friends with a horror story. "This entire area is mined. Nobody knows exactly where the mines are, because in the monsoon season the rains shift them. That's why the soldiers need to go and look for them periodically."

"I bet at such times they can't cope with all the volunteers," said Chuck. He lifted his hand as though trying to attract attention and spoke: "Please let *me* go, sir! Oh, please let it be me! I want to be blown up for my country!"

A lorry went by carrying a detachment of glum-faced soldiers in camouflage gear who might be on their way to look for mines. It seemed as if the proximity of the Demilitarised Zone had caused the South Koreans to pile as many men and weapons as possible into the area in a last-ditch attempt. The large building that greeted us in a clearing on the side of the hill was once again being guarded by soldiers, and when we parked amongst the vehicles waiting outside and went in, I learnt from an inscription in English on a wall that the premises belonged to the First Division of the Army of the Republic of Korea.

"This place used to be called the Hall of Anti-communism," said Moon, "now it's called the Hall of Peace. You'll be watching a film; I'll see you later."

Chuck, Blossom and I went into a lecture hall where a handful of foreigners brought by other tour companies were waiting in orange plastic chairs, and sat down. When the lights dimmed, the title "Third Assault Tunnel" appeared on the screen in front of us, followed by a sequence of images accompanied by the voice of a female narrator with an American accent. Apparently, in 1974 the South Koreans had discovered a tunnel dug under the Ceasefire Line by Northerners. Within months of the discovery of this passage, believed to be for use in a future assault, a second tunnel had come to light, but the third tunnel, found four years later, had caused greater consternation because of its being both much larger and much closer to Seoul.

According to the film, Southerners had developed a special technique for looking for tunnels. Geological measurements were used to determine the likely location of a tunnel, and then a hole was bored in the ground and water was shot into it under pressure. If it failed to jet back up, it was assumed there was a tunnel below. The next step was to estimate the point the tunnel had reached, and, at a spot a little beyond that, start a "counter tunnel" which, descending at a certain angle would eventually cut its way into the tunnel that was being looked for. This was how the Third Assault Tunnel, whose existence was revealed by a defector from the North, was found. The film, which spent a lot of time showing the inside of the tunnel that resembled a mining gallery, concluded with a section on the discovery, in 1990, of a fourth tunnel which, although located further from Seoul, was even bigger.

When we went out, Moon found us again as she had promised and, handing each of us a glossy brochure called "Undermining the Foundations of Peace", said, "We'll go and see the tunnel itself as well, but first we are going to the Observatory."

The Observatory, built to gaze not at the stars but North Korea, was at the summit of the hill. The squat concrete building didn't seem very big from the outside, but as soon as we went in, it was revealed that this impression was deceptive. When Moon pushed the double doors open we found ourselves on the top tier of an amphitheatre similar to a lecture room in a university, with a giant wall made entirely of glass in front of us. I realised this was as far as we could go in South Korea: the Demilitarised Zone was in the broad green valley at the foot of the steep slope on which the glass wall sat, and, beyond that, North Korea began. At the bottom of the amphitheatre, a few visitors were listening to the commentary being delivered by a sergeant who, like all his comrades, was in camouflage gear, whilst other visitors stood at the telescopes situated along the glass wall, gazing at the structures belonging to the North in the valley and on the slopes opposite.

When we got to the bottom ourselves, I heard the sergeant saying, with a rhythm that suggested he had memorised his words, "The Demilitarised Zone is four kilometres wide, with an electrified fence on either side, and the Ceasefire Line goes right down the middle. Ahead, you can see

Panmunjom, which sits on the Ceasefire Line. That's where the peace talks between us take place. But occasionally there are other developments inside the negotiation area. You may have heard that in 1976 two American soldiers were hacked to death there by Northerners with an axe. We and the North each have a village in the Demilitarised Zone, but no one actually lives in theirs. Every night they put on lights in those buildings over there to make us think there are people in them, but the lights always come on and go off at exactly the same time." He gestured towards the high-rise blocks, not all that different from those in Seoul, that could just about be made out amongst the hills on the other side of the valley. "Those are the outskirts of Kaesong, the second largest city in the North. If there are any Northerners living around here, that's where they are."

Chuck and Blossom had found a pair of telescopes that had become vacant and were looking at the places the sergeant was talking about. I, too, put my eye to the end of a vacant telescope and saw, with a hallucinatory clarity through the powerful lens, Panmunjom, the fake Northern village and the rusting carcass of a steam engine left over from the war beside a railway line in the buffer zone that no longer went anywhere. Then I trained the telescope on the high-rises of Kaesong kilometres away.

As we were leaving the Observatory, Chuck, running his hand through his thinning hair, said to Blossom, in his usual effort to share his happiness, "What did you think? It was interesting, wasn't it?" Then he turned to me and asked: "Did you know about that axe attack?"

Because Moon was hovering nearby with an expression on her face that said she was pleased with what she had been able to show us, and I didn't want her to think once again that I was a European who knew everything, I said, "No" and then listened to Chuck's chatter and jokes in the minibus all through the brief journey through narrow roads to the Third Assault Tunnel.

Although the "counter tunnel" at the entrance was dug at quite a sharp angle, because the assault tunnel was a considerable way below the surface, we had to walk downhill for a long time between the electric lights on either side. We finally reached the passage resembling a mining gallery we had seen in the film at the Hall of Peace and walked on, listening to the voices of tour guides echoing from the rough walls. Here and there, Northerners had erected concrete columns to support the ceiling, and when their excavations were discovered they had painted these to resemble rocks in a bid to make the tunnel appear like a natural structure. The section open to the public ended about five hundred metres further on at a thick steel screen, in front of which two soldiers sat with a field telephone between them, gazing through narrow slits into the darkness ahead, from whose depths a Northern attack could still materialise.

When we returned to the surface, Moon said we were free to wander about by ourselves for ten or fifteen minutes until we went to lunch, and she left to let the restaurant know that we were on our way. Once again, soldiers stood here and there, and at one end there was a military-looking, single-storey building I hadn't noticed when we arrived. When, after making my way to a group of dusty trees and walking under them for a while, I turned round to take another look at the mouth of the tunnel, I saw Chuck and Blossom talking to a young officer in the distance, and because there was something about the way they held themselves that suggested things weren't quite right, I went over and joined them.

Not noticing a sign that said "No photography", Blossom had been caught filming, like a real spy, a hoarding showing the route of the tunnel with the video camera she had bought with her earnings in Singapore, and now the cassette was jammed and she was having difficulty rewinding it to hand it over to the officer for confiscation. Like other Chinese I had seen before in a rage, she looked not agitated but in a state of icy calm. She was speaking, but it was as if her words were issuing from behind a wall of silence and making the existence of that barrier all the more obvious.

"Since the Northerners dug the tunnel in the first place, don't they know its route anyway?" I asked.

"What matters is that they shouldn't know what we know," replied the officer solemnly. "If something like this came out, we could lose twenty to thirty thousand men."

I was tired of this absurd game. Northerners switched on lights in empty houses and painted pictures of rocks on concrete, while Southerners walked about amongst this cheap stage scenery, waving their arms and shouting "We could have thousands of casualties" like ham actors, and from time to time someone was chopped to pieces with an axe or got blown up while looking for mines.

At least the incident had put Chuck in an even better humour. As the three of us were walking over to the minibus after Blossom had broken off the jammed cassette and given it to the officer, he said, "Don't worry; if you'd ended up in jail I'd have brought you a file and a rope ladder baked in a cake."

But by the time we reached the restaurant, he appeared to be in a more serious mood. After we crossed our legs and sat down at the low Korean table to which Moon had conducted us before leaving to eat separately with Mr Lee, he said, "I believe that, despite everything, the whole world will be a single country and live in brotherhood one day."

"Is that the official view of the US Navy?"

He ignored me. "Why not? Communism's collapsed, the Berlin Wall's down. People are coming together all over the place." He put his arm around Blossom's shoulder. "I believe that when we get married it'll be a step forward for world peace."

I could now see the cracks that would eventually lead to the collapse of his happiness. Apart from the fact that the only lesson that could possibly be drawn from all that we had seen since the morning was that mankind was not heading towards universal brotherhood, it was also far from certain that he and Blossom would get married. It was obvious that she didn't like the way Chuck disclosed everything from the amount of money he had to his mother's wishes, and tried to demonstrate the intimacy between the two of them to everyone they encountered. They were essentially an ill-matched couple. He was one of those naïve, optimistic Americans with a firm belief that every stranger is potentially a friend and every problem has a solution, whom I had spent my youth mocking and could now recognise as better and nicer human beings than myself. She, on the other hand, had grown up in a country where life had been hard and dangerous for centuries, and people understandably approached the world with suspicion. And as if that wasn't enough, there was something hard in her own personality. Not only because she sat directly behind me in the minibus and was overshadowed by the boisterous Chuck, but also because of her tendency to hide herself, it had taken me a long time to form a real impression of her, but her response to the officer demanding the cassette from her video recorder had finally shown me the sort of person she was. Behind the hardness she had displayed then, as behind the strength that had enabled her to learn English and get out of China, there might lurk a woman who could dispassionately weigh what an American sailor could give her against what, say, a Singaporean doctor could. Because I had taken a liking to Chuck and didn't want to think about these things any more, I busied myself with the pickles and the transparent soup put down before me.

It was half past two by the time the meal was over, and half past three by the time the minibus was approaching the city. As Chuck and Blossom wanted to spend their last evening in Seoul at the centre, I was going to be dropped off first at my hotel. Shaking her hair with the red highlights in it, Moon had once again begun to hum a pop song.

"It was a very instructive day for me," Chuck said. "They keep telling us about North Korea in Japan. I am glad I saw it all with my own eyes. If I have as good a time in Thailand I won't have any right to complain."

"Oh, you are young," said Moon. "You'll have a good time in many places yet." It seemed as if she had suddenly stopped being merry and lapsed into an end-of-the-day melancholy.

"What do you mean I am young?" Chuck replied. "You are the same age as me."

"Yes, but in Korea if you've reached the age of twenty-eight and are still unmarried you are considered old."

"It's the same in Japan. No Japanese woman can get married after she's thirty. She could get married to a foreigner of course, but never to a Japanese."

Moon looked at him with an expression that said "See!" and then, turning to me, "How do you think I could get married?" she asked.

I wasn't altogether surprised at the emergence of this topic. Although it appeared to me to have come up suddenly, it was obviously permanently on her mind and was what lay behind her childish behaviour. But I was still a little taken aback to discover she was quite a bit older than I had thought. "If you want to get married, I'm sure you can," I told her, and immediately regretted it. By uttering this polite remark which served no useful purpose I had indeed behaved like a European.

But Chuck was an American who believed in practical solutions. "I have a friend who's being transferred to Korea," he said. "Give me your phone number and I'll get him to call you when he arrives; maybe you'll get on."

Moon covered her mouth with her hand and giggled as though she were, not a twenty-eight-year-old woman, but an eight-year-old girl. "I can't, I'd be embarrassed, embarrassed," she said.

"Then try the internet; we two met in a chatroom."

It was obvious that Blossom found this revelation about her being the kind of woman who trawls through cyberspace for men particularly unseemly. Her silence radiating from behind me was virtually dense enough to reach out and touch: I had no doubt they'd be quarrelling that evening.

When I recognised the buildings ahead and realised we were approaching my hotel, I reached for my jacket with relief.

"How did you know we had arrived?" Moon asked.

"I am European, I know everything," I replied and then was afraid she might think I was mocking not myself but her. But she'd already forgotten me and begun thinking of the husband she'd never marry, the children she'd never have, the days she'd spend taking such foreigners as came to Seoul from place to place.

When the minibus came to a stop, "*Kamsahamnida*," I murmured to her, using one of the Korean phrases I had picked up, before twisting round and saying "Nice meeting you" to Chuck and Blossom.

"And you," replied Chuck.

"Yes, and you," echoed Blossom, looking at me as if to say, "These two are a pair of idiots, but you seem to be someone who notices what is going on around you; that's why I want you to go."

I opened the door and got out. As Mr Lee, the only one who had not uttered a single word all day, drove the minibus away like a mythological ferryman taking the dead to Hades,

I stood on the steps and looked at its receding shape for a few seconds, thinking I would never see any of them again. Then I turned round and went inside.

* * *

The train I boarded for Busan towards noon the next day boasted a degree of luxury no longer offered by trains or any other mode of transport in the West. The wide red plush seats reclined at the touch of a button, the reading lights above could be adjusted, and at the end of the carriage there was a large video screen providing information in Korean and English. It was hard to believe that the fare for the four-and-a-half-hour journey didn't even come to 25,000 won.

At precisely the appointed time we smoothly slid forward, left the Seoul Tower and the back of Namsan, till then visible from the windows, behind us and, gathering speed as we trundled across a steel bridge over the Han, began making our way south. The endless high-rises of Seoul were eventually succeeded by towns with broad avenues. Apart from Protestant churches built of brick and old Korean stone houses with curved roofs here and there, everything seemed to be made of concrete. The signs in Hangul characters looked as if they were fighting with one another for space between the buildings, and because telephone lines, instead of being expensively laid underground, hung in sagging arcs between stark poles as in America, the overall effect compared unfavourably with the featurelessness of Seoul which at least had the virtue of being accompanied by tidiness.

Yet, beyond all this was a landscape made up of steep green hills with broad valleys between them. Whenever I took my eyes off manmade structures I could believe we were travelling through Austria or Switzerland. This must have been a beautiful land when the first Mongolian tribes had arrived here on horseback to begin their long transformation into Koreans. And in all probability it had remained beautiful until its unfortunate exposure to Western influences in the late nineteenth century.

A white crane stood absolutely still, waiting for fish to catch by a brook that was shallow enough for its bed to be visible. Two men sitting in chairs in a market garden waved as the train went by. After our only stop Tejon, where, once again, we arrived precisely on time and stayed for only a minute, the hills got higher and the tiny spotlessly clean stations with blue-tiled roofs we hurtled through without stopping became increasingly alpine in appearance, as though they should have been called Bensheim or Kleinbach. It was through a series of mountain passes that we actually descended to Busan shortly after four o'clock.

In the hotel I found directly in the large square in front of the station there were signs in the Cyrillic alphabet everywhere as if Russian guests were expected. When I got into the lift, which was painted gold inside, I found that the floor numbers skipped from 3 to 5. Although I had frequently heard that, because the words for "four" and "death" sounded similar, fourth floors were considered unlucky, and therefore omitted, in parts of the Far East, this was the first time I was witnessing the practice for myself.

Because of the mode of counting involved, my room was actually not on the sixth but the fifth floor. The carved pink roses on the headboards of the two beds and the purple carpet on the floor seemed to have been chosen by the same interior decorator who had gold-plated the lift. None of this, though, was particularly important in a place where I would be spending all of two nights. Without giving it any further thought, I left my holdall in the bottom of the wardrobe, made my way back downstairs and went out.

At first glance Busan, Korea's second city with its population of four million, appeared to be just a smaller version of Seoul. There were no skyscrapers, but the same buildings of a few storeys stood at the foot of the hills, giving way to the same tall apartment blocks on the slopes. Apart from being blue instead of yellow, the plastic water tanks on every building were identical to those in the capital, and the same applied to the buses, which were green-and-white instead of orange-and-white. And here, too, there were interconnecting subways which were in fact shop-lined arcades.

Then I began noticing that the city had a few features of its own as well. Unlike Seoul, located thirty kilometres inland from the Yellow Sea, Busan, located at the point the Sea of Japan met the Pacific, smelt not of cooking fat but of salt water and was filled with the dense, honey-tinted light of the ocean. Because it was so much further to the south, it also had a sprinkling of exotic-looking trees and shrubs amidst more common varieties in its parks. Much more striking than all this, though, was the presence everywhere of signs in Cyrillic characters like the ones in my hotel, spelling out messages in Russian.

When the owners of a shop I was walking past came out and tried to speak to me in the same language, I looked at the signs more carefully and, relying on the few shreds of knowledge left to me from an attempt I had made long ago to learn Russian, managed to decipher that many of them featured the words *Rossiskiye* and *matros*. I still remembered the latter meant "seaman": it had to be that Russian ships called regularly at this busy port, with crew members immediately rushing out for an extensive shopping trip at bargain prices, followed by a stay somewhere like my hotel for those granted overnight shore leave. A Second Officer or a Chief Engineer named Sergei or Ilya might have leaned against the carved pink roses I would be leaning against that evening. Later,

I also came across a Russian restaurant named the Balalaika in a side street, and three Russian-looking young women in very short skirts stood outside a bar, chewing gum. It seemed the USO in Seoul were not the only ones ready to comfort those who were away from home.

Despite the virtually subtropical greenery I had seen, at the harbour a harsh wind blew in from the sea, tossing the squawking seagulls about the sky. That, though, didn't stop me from walking out on to the bridge connecting Busan to Yongdo Island to look at the freighters and fishing boats on either side and the containers marked "Hyundai", "Hanjin" and "Evergreen" on the wharves.

By the time I started heading back it was getting dark. The city had put on its lights and those leaving work were queuing up at stops for the green-and-white buses. Arriving at my hotel towards a quarter past seven after making my way through the homebound crowds in the streets with a certain sense of loneliness, I spotted the inscription "Four Seasons Restaurant" on a first-floor window. Having had nothing but Korean-style meals for days, always starting with the same kimchi plate and clear soup, I was beginning to need Western food for a change. Thinking an establishment with such a name might be the place to get it, I went up in the golden lift.

The restaurant, with dark wood panelling on the walls, was dimly lit and almost empty. Two male patrons in their early twenties were smoking and talking in hushed tones at one table, and nearby a middle-aged man was sitting with an attractive girl. Perhaps this was one of Busan's fashionable spots and I was witnessing a seduction attempt. I sat down at a window-side table, chose a pork chop from the menu brought by a waiter young enough almost to be considered a child and, after hesitating for a second, asked for a bottle of white wine as well.

It seemed that the fact that I wasn't having a Korean or Chinese meal was not going to change anything. "Kimchi?" asked the waiter.

"No."

He was clearly disturbed by this departure from tradition. "Soup?" he tried with a wrinkled brow.

"No, just the chop."

Without saying anything, he picked up the menu and disappeared through a door by the bar behind which rows of bottles gleamed on shelves. When he returned a few minutes later, the wine he brought in an ice bucket was accompanied by the kimchi plate I had turned down. Thinking objecting wouldn't do any good, I filled my glass and popped some pickle in my mouth. I could see the green lights on the roofs of the taxis at the rank below. Passengers on their way to night trains were walking through the square. In the speech bubble coming out of the mouth of the smiling man on the video hoarding opposite, Hangul characters unfurled to praise the advertised product.

By the time the chop arrived smothered in a thick brown sauce, I had finished my second glass and started on the third. The two diners in their twenties were still talking and the middle-aged man was still trying to seduce his companion. As in the hotel's Cyrillic signs and failed décor, in this mournful restaurant, too, there was something reminiscent of the old Iron Curtain countries. If there had been a woman in a silver dress singing out-of-fashion songs in English into an ancient microphone with a cord, the picture would have been complete.

As if this thought had communicated itself to the management and, in the absence of a *chanteuse*, a different expedient had been hit upon, a quarter of an hour later, as I was finishing my chop, a music system was turned on somewhere and Tom Jones's "The Green Green Grass of Home" filled the room. I imagined Jones, a resident of the United States for more than three decades, singing this song about the beauty of his native Wales to American matrons on a gambling trip in a Las Vegas hotel. The plastic America of those women, the incredibly green fields of the British Isles and the small flat in Istanbul where I had first heard the song myself years earlier on the radio flooded into my mind at the same time. It was as if I had lost something in one of them and could find it again only if I made a real effort to look for it. But I had to look for whatever it was I had lost not in one of these three places but somewhere else, perhaps at the bottom of the glass in my hand. It was one of those moments when everything is utterly clear, but just can't be put into words.

Suddenly I realised I was drunk. To get drunk by myself in a dark city by the Sea of Japan where miniskirted Russian whores roamed the streets was not a good idea. Deciding not to finish the two fingers of wine left in the bottle, I stood up and, conscious of swaying slightly, walked towards the exit.

The woman at the till was singing softly along with Tom Jones, but her accent had turned "The green green grass of home" into "The clean clean glass of home". Asking her to put the dinner on my account, I made my way to my room, sat down on the edge of the bed and, looking at the carved wooden roses, began wondering if taking a shower would sober me up.

* * *

When I opened my eyes in the morning I had a headache. Thinking sea air might help, I got dressed quickly and left the hotel. At the harbour it was only slightly less windy than on the previous day. After wandering about for a while, I found myself in a maze of cobbled alleys lined with fishmongers and seafood restaurants. Crates containing fish, crabs and lobsters were stacked up against the whitewashed walls. In front of the shops, women wearing surgical caps and heavy-duty rubber gloves were gutting the morning's catch into buckets rapidly filling with blood and silvery scales, while inside, men sat drinking tea and watching sporting events on portable TV sets.

My headache hadn't got any better. If anything, the smell of the fish market had made it worse, but there wasn't much I could do. As the next day would be taken up first with returning to Seoul and then packing in preparation for leaving Korea the following morning, this was effectively the last day of my trip, so I had to make use of it. Deciding to go and see Pomosa, said to be one of the finest temples in the country, I took the underground to the northern edge of the city.

The road outside the station where I got off the train still had a pavement on both sides, but it was obvious that it would soon ditch these and, leaving behind the last buildings of Busan, become a proper highway leading to whatever conurbation was next. Following a sign in Latin characters that pointed in the direction of Pomosa, I turned left, walked past a group of houses once again reminiscent of the Alps and began following a mountain road winding up through a beech wood.

Not even the darkness and the quiet under the trees had managed to dull my headache, and when I saw a second sign that said "Pomosa 3 km" I began wondering how much longer I could go on. But minutes later I was overtaken by a white lorry smaller than a passenger car, which came to a stop a short distance ahead. A young man in glasses then stuck his head out of the window and said, "Where are you going?"

"To the temple."

"I'm taking a delivery there myself. You can come with me if you wish."

Thanking him, I climbed into the passenger seat. His English was fluent and we began talking.

"Where are you from?" he asked.

"Turkey."

"I've never met anyone from Turkey before. What are you doing in Korea?

"Just travelling. I was in Seoul for four days and this is my second day in Busan, but tomorrow I'll set out to go back."

"To Turkey?"

"No, to England."

He looked at me.

"I live in England," I explained.

"Now I understand."

But, being from a place where the few foreign visitors that turned up tended to be Russian sailors looking for fake designer t-shirts and sunglasses and genuine Korean electronic goods, he clearly didn't find a Turk living in England easy to understand. Turning to something he was more familiar with, he said, "The temple is beautiful; you'll like it. Whenever I'm there it fills me with peace and I feel completely at home."

It was obvious that three kilometres was not an inconsiderable distance even for a motor vehicle. After climbing amongst the beeches for some time, we were joined on the left by a stream that foamed against rocks as it rushed down the slope, and then our path was blocked by a metal pole like the barrier at a border crossing.

The words in Korean uttered by the guard who emerged from his hut were translated by my friend in glasses as "You have to pay 1,000 won."

He seemed to be embarrassed that they were charging for entry into the temple, but it didn't bother me. I handed over a brown 1,000-won note, itself with a picture of a temple on the back. The guard lifted the barrier and we drove through.

After about a hundred metres we reached a piece of level ground where my friend stopped the lorry, saying, "This is as far as I go. If you keep walking you'll soon see the temple.

Heading in the direction he indicated, I reached a second piece of level ground, this one paved, and bordered by not the single structure I had expected but a whole series of open-fronted temples, and behind these a set of steps led to a third piece of level ground with another such series. The ancient buildings constructed of stone and wood were not unimpressive with their curved roofs against the high green hills in the background. If the Korean authorities ever decided to try to attract tourists to their country, this would doubtless be the sort of place featured on their travel posters.

I climbed up the steps to the third piece of level ground. In the smallest of the temples, plunged into silence except for a bell gently tinkling by itself outside in the breeze, a handful of people were meditating in the lotus position, and some distance away a more complex ritual was in progress in one of the bigger buildings. A shaven-headed priest in a long orange robe facing a gold-painted statue of Buddha periodically struck a wooden gong he was holding as the congregation kneeling behind him bowed and rose, murmuring a chant that sounded like *Nam chem bozai*. The shoes of the worshippers stood in front of the door and rows of much smaller Buddhas, each holding a lightbulb representing a candle, filled the shelves of the cabinet behind the golden statue. Obviously, Buddhism, which the American missionaries had done their best to suppress, still resonated with some. Even here, though, contrary to Western assumptions, a relentless realism was at work, and there were offerings of fruit everywhere as though to emphasise that even gods had to eat. Closing my eyes, I, too, murmured "*Nam chem bozai*" over and over again together with everyone else for a while, but, as

I had expected, felt not like someone who had arrived at his spiritual home but only a traveller passing through.

It was after one o'clock when I finally left the temple grounds. Although the road was downhill all the way, it took me nearly another three quarters of an hour to walk the three kilometres to the outskirts of Busan and by the time I had had some tea there at a small café as a belated substitute for my missed breakfast, and made the long underground journey back to the city centre, it was late afternoon. But there were still hours of daylight left for wandering about, so when I spotted a sign that said "Yondusan Park" I followed it.

Like the park on top of Namsan Hill in Seoul, this park on top of a hill overlooking Busan, too, seemed dominated by a tower; but, in keeping with the rule of everything here being on a smaller scale than its equivalent in the capital, the structure I could see as I approached my destination was shorter and reminiscent more of an airport control tower than a spacecraft.

Just inside the park gates a small middle-aged group were dancing on one side to music from a CD-player placed on a low wall. The Far Eastern love of dance was something I had witnessed before, but, unlike the couples I had seen gliding gracefully in Kowloon Park in Hong Kong one morning as a similar CD-player poured out waltzes, this group were engaged in what looked like a particularly energetic Korean version of rock 'n' roll. For a while I stood there, watching the men and women, all of them over fifty, shaking their arms and legs. Then I moved on and walked past the old men playing *go* on the benches under a row of gingko trees a little further ahead without paying any attention to the dancers.

In the middle of the main part of the park there was a large circular flowerbed surrounded by a low railing. The bushes behind this barrier were pruned into perfect spheres and at the centre of the inner circle they formed was a high plinth on which stood a black statue of Admiral Yi which was either a replica or a close imitation of the one at the Gwanghwamun Intersection. The aged sailor who had defeated the Japanese with his turtle ships still seemed to be keeping a watchful eye on his old enemies from this hill by the waters where he had won his great victory.

I climbed up to the next level and, standing with my back to the tower, gazed out at the sea myself over Yi's head. The sky was cloudless as though scoured clean by the wind over the last two days. Under the soft afternoon sun reaching into every corner, the dazzling blue of the Pacific, the red bridge to Yongdo Island and the white high-rises climbing up the green hills on the opposite shore were visible with an astonishing clarity, and, like a soundtrack created to accompany it all, from below there still came faint strains of rock 'n' roll music.

For the first time in days I was confronted by a scene of real beauty, and my headache was largely gone, too; but none of it seemed to make much difference, and it wasn't because I knew that what I was seeing was not typical. Perhaps because Korea was further off the beaten track than some of the other places I had been to, I had become more aware than ever on this trip that I no longer had any real roots or a home anywhere. The next day I would take a train to Seoul with provincial housewives on a shopping spree, businessmen in grey suits, and Korean punks with orange hair. Then I would go to Amsterdam, followed by London, followed by somewhere else, and things would go on in this way for years to come. Nor was I really looking for something, as I had believed the night before in the midst of my drunkenness. My possessions were reduced to a few memories from my childhood and youth, and the strange pleasure I still derived from words, from knowing that *Kamsahamnida* meant "thank you" in Korean, and *matros* was Russian for "sailor". Wrapped in these as in some kind of armour, I was aimlessly wandering about the world. Korea might appear featureless and static at times but the one truly so, the man always on the move but never reaching anywhere other than yet another Gwanghwamun Intersection with an assortment of wild roads radiating from it that each bore a different name but led to an equally alien destination was me.

Looking at the city below lying under the sun, I ran all this through my mind without feeling a great deal. A white ferry was leaving the harbour to sail to Japan. I watched it until it vanished from sight behind one of Yondo's distant headlands, but I didn't wonder, as I would once have done, if one day I, too, would go to Japan. Instead, the way I had looked at Seoul from the cable car on my first day in the country, I went on looking at the sea left empty by the disappearance of the ferry.

THE BLUE LOTUS

The tail-engined plane was more than half empty. The two stewardesses in navy-blue uniforms did not reappear once they cleared away the breakfast trays they had handed out as soon as we were airborne. After shining weakly on the flat rice paddies below throughout the two-hour flight, the January sun, too, withdrew as we were approaching our destination; we landed on the grey tarmac through a grey rain.

I got into one of the battered taxis of indeterminate make waiting outside the terminal and uttered the name I had been told my hotel was locally known by: "*Heping Fandian*".

Without saying anything, the driver started the engine. Leaving behind the rundown European-style villas of a district built by the old foreign settlers, we entered a muddy motorway. Dirty plastic sheeting fluttered under the rain between the metal rods protruding from the raised concrete strip that ran down the centre. Old buses, overloaded lorries, police vehicles with flashing red and blue lights and the odd car went past. By the side of the road, industrial areas alternated with high-rise collective housing.

Some twenty minutes later, the pewtery light that indicates the presence of a body of water loomed ahead out of the rain. Not long afterwards, we exited the motorway via a ramp gently descending on pillars and I saw the wide, ashen river with freighters and passenger ships anchored in the middle of it. On the opposite bank giant construction cranes were building a new city of postmodern skyscrapers, and a little further away was a steel tower even taller than these structures. On an enormous tripod an equally enormous sphere had been placed, and the body of the tower soared above this, holding up a smaller sphere capped by a transmission mast with its upper part lost in the rainclouds above.

When I turned my eyes to the side of the river we were on I had the feeling that a flickering black-and-white newsreel from the 1930s had come to life. The grey stone buildings which, unlike the unfinished skyscrapers opposite, aped the West not of today but seventy years ago, no longer housed the banks and companies whose property they had once been. But the old columns, carvings, reliefs, domes and clock towers were all still there in the murky afternoon. I was reminded of the words spoken by my childhood hero Tintin in *The Blue Lotus* on stepping ashore from an ocean liner on another rainy day at this very spot: "So this is Shanghai!"

It was indeed here that vanished notorious city wrested from its rightful owners and carved up between the major Western powers had lived and breathed in its free-for-all Wild East heyday. If old Shanghai, deserving some credit for giving sanctuary to refugees like the grandparents of Sergei Andreyevich, whom I had met on the jetfoil from Macao to Hong Kong two years earlier, but rightly better known for offering the sufficiently unscrupulous a chance to build a shady career against a backdrop of brothels, gambling joints and opium dens, could be represented by a single location, I was currently at it. This road, known as the Bund, by the Yangtze's impressive tributary the Huangpu, had been the main artery of the International Settlement where foreign nationals from all over the world had lived outside Chinese jurisdiction, protected by British and American troops with some assistance from Sikh policemen imported from India. Meanwhile, the French had held sway in their own "Concession" a few kilometres away, and this way of life had not fully ended until Mao's People's Liberation Army had turned up at the gates in 1949. As well as draining the local swamps and building a high embankment by the river to protect the Bund from the periodic flooding it had suffered till then, the Communists had addressed their efforts to the moral swamp around them, tackling every form of vice with puritanical efficiency till economic stagnation had presented them with another swamp forty years later and they had been forced to turn for assistance to the heirs of the foreign capitalists they had driven away. Now Shanghai was a metropolis pursuing money in a more disciplined way and trying to catch up with the other big cities of the Far East.

The Cathay, once perhaps the most famous hotel in the Orient, was still on the corner of the Bund and Nanjing Road, its twelve-storey body under a high, pyramid-shaped copper roof, oxidised long ago to green, as gracefully slim as ever, but its name now changed to the Peace Hotel. When the driver stopped the taxi, I took my holdall, went up the steps and walked through the door held open by a uniformed doorman with a "Welcome, sir" uttered in a heavy American accent.

The man at Reception was studying the red Japanese passport with a stylised chrysanthemum on it handed to him by a young woman in an expensive-looking long black coat. Clearly, the Japanese, who had gone even further than Westerners in seizing chunks of China in the old days, were now coming back with the present Western influx. I waited for the woman to take her passport and leave before getting the man to find the reservation I had made from Beijing. The lift he directed me to was empty; I went up to my room, left my holdall among the furniture from no period in particular but dark and heavy enough to reflect the hotel's "historic" past, and, returning downstairs, walked out into Nanjing Road.

A short distance away a man, identifiable by his prominent cheekbones and less than fully slanted eyes as an Uighur from Xinjiang, stood in a doorway watching the rain, which had let up a bit. As I went past he whispered, "Change money?" taking care not to look at me. Not looking at him myself, I declined his offer with a lift of my shoulders and kept going.

The pot-holed, muddy pavements were crowded enough to testify to the fact that I was in a city with a population of almost fifteen million. Most people were dressed in clothes that could be seen anywhere in the world, but a few who were in blue Mao suits and matching caps indicated that the Cultural Revolution was not yet completely forgotten. What the two groups had in common was the undisguised curiosity with which they stared at me as though even in this big city they were not accustomed to coming across foreigners.

Taxis similar to the one I had taken from the airport and articulated trolleybuses went down the road. At a crossroads the traffic was being directed by a policeman standing, like his counterparts in the Istanbul of my childhood, inside a metal cylinder going up to his waist on top of a circular wooden platform. When the policeman put his whistle to his lips and blew, the dozens of cyclists waiting at the mouth of the road to the left flowed past me with parcels, baskets and bundles strapped behind them, amidst a whirring of wheels and ringing of bells. "So this is Shanghai!" I thought again. After years, I, too, was finally about to encounter the Blue Lotus.

Here and there stood a McDonald's, Burger King or Pizza Hut displaying posters and menus in Chinese, and walls were covered in advertisements for international brands. But the grey stone façades of some of the biggest shops looked as outdated as their quaint names such as Number Ten Department Store and Number One Shanghai Provisions

Company written in English, and in front of them there were stalls on the pavement selling cheap silk scarves and jade trinkets. The narrow side streets I gazed down offered even less, being lined mainly with ramshackle dwellings of a few storeys interspersed with tiny repair shops and eateries: if Shanghai was serious about reaching the same level as other Far Eastern cities, many of them well ahead of the West, a great leap forward would be required.

Outside a Holiday Inn whose green neon sign gleamed dully behind the rain, another man with prominent cheekbones and skin browned into leather on the steppes pretended to be deeply interested in something on the opposite pavement as he murmured, "Change money?" Uighurs seemed to have cornered the foreign-currency black market.

On a street corner a boy of sixteen or seventeen stood, holding out an elaborately detailed model of a warship made of unpainted tin. I had seen people silently trying to sell such models in Beijing, too. Suddenly I became conscious of missing Beijing. I had looked on it as a mere stepping stone to Shanghai, which I had expected to be the more interesting of the two, and the wide boulevards, the Ministries sporting the red emblem of the People's Republic with the yellow stars on it, the pagodas and artificial lakes in the parks, the adults flying fish- and dragon-shaped kites in Tiananmen Square in the early evening with the joy of children, the mannequins in the clothing shops in Wangfujing Road with the faces and hairdos of Western women of fifty years earlier but, in concession to Chinese physique, only two-thirds as big as similar mannequins still to be found in the British provinces, and even the Great Wall of China, a mere sixty kilometres outside the city, had not made much of an impression on me, or perhaps only made an impression of not making an impression. Compared to the greyness and gloom of Shanghai, though, all these now seemed to belong to a brighter and more spacious world.

The short winter day was ending. Yellow lights had come on in the shops, and neon signs composed of Chinese characters had begun to flash here and there. Deciding to return to my hotel, I crossed over to the other side under the rain.

People continued to stare at me. At a jade stall illuminated by naked lightbulbs, a man pointed to a sign that said "25 yuan" before holding up a necklace and training the tall flame from the lighter in his other hand on the beads to show they were not plastic and didn't melt. But I shook my head and kept walking.

Before long I felt a touch on my arm and, turning round, discovered a young girl had appeared beside me. "May I walk with you? I'd like to practice my English," she said.

If her make-up and the slits in her skirt visible under her short coat hadn't both been so excessive, she could indeed have passed for a language student. "There's no need," I told her, "your English sounds good enough already."

For a moment her scarlet mouth twisted in anger as if she was about to object, but then she shrugged and walked away.

The next hand to grab hold of my arm was bigger and stronger. Its owner, a gaunt-looking young man, had only a woollen jacket on despite the rain.

"I'm Peter," he said briefly.

I had never been able to work out where the Western names used by the Chinese came from. Did his real name sound like "Peter"? Or was "Peter" actually one of his names? Or did he perhaps simply use different Western names at different times?

Paying no attention to the fact that I hadn't reciprocated with my own name, "Where are you from?" he went on to ask.

Rather than going into a long explanation, "England," I replied.

"Where are you staying?"

"At the Peace Hotel."

He nodded in a way that indicated he approved of my choice. "It's good. It used to be almost the only good hotel in the city, but now we've got many: Shanghai's improving."

"I've noticed."

"And where are you going to eat tonight?"

Because I could guess what would follow such a question, "I don't know," I said. "I was travelling earlier in the day, so I'm a bit tired. I might just have something in my room."

"There's a very good restaurant I know. We could go there and then I could give you a massage at my place."

"Thank you, but no. As I said, I am tired." And suddenly I felt genuinely tired and, not caring that I was being rude, quickened my pace so that he was left behind.

Here and there shutters were noisily coming down. When I spotted another girl ahead who looked as if she might want to practice her English, I crossed back to the other side and after walking for while on the muddy pavements, looking at the shops and the stalls that were still open, I reached the Peace Hotel.

From this angle, the steel tower on the other side of the river looked as if it was immediately at the bottom of the road. It was floodlit, but, veiled by the evening mist rising from the waters, was more of a luminous bulk than a distinct shape. The part that could be made out most clearly was the enormous sphere on top of the tripod which had its outline traced by the small lights flashing on it. There was something vaguely eerie about it all, like a sequence in a science fiction film featuring an alien spacecraft silently signalling in an attempt to establish contact with earth. It was as if another world was calling to Shanghai through the darkness and the rain. For a moment I gazed at the scene, then, deciding to eat in my room as I had told Peter, I went up.

* * *

In the morning, the rain had stopped, but the day was still cold and overcast. On the corner of the Bund a woman who had a small plastic holdall beside her on the ground was selling city maps for 1 yuan. I went down the subway steps she was standing next to and walked over to the other side. The long green strip where I emerged was dotted with flowerbeds and food kiosks along its length, and near the spot where I found myself there was a bronze statue of Mao some five or six metres high. His face turned to the East, he was marching purposefully, with his right hand raised as though to say "Follow me!" Above his head, red flags fluttered on a row of even taller poles.

I located the steps leading to the top of the broad embankment built to protect the Bund and joined the Chinese taking their morning walk, wrapped in heavy coats against the weather. On the opposite bank the top of the steel tower was once again lost in the clouds. Cranes were swivelling right and left as they built the Shanghai of the new century. In the middle of the river a tug towed a long line of coal barges strapped together two by two. A white passenger ship with rust streaks on her side was moving in the direction of the Yangtze in preparation for sailing hundreds of miles into the interior of China.

When I turned to look at the old buildings along the Bund, I saw that a few of them also had a red flag flying from its roof like the ones above Mao's head. One building had turned into a Kentucky Fried Chicken branch: framed menus hung on either side of the door, accompanied on the left by a large figure of Colonel Sanders, the goateed and bespectacled founder of the chain, in his trademark Southern gentleman's garb of white suit and black shoestring bow tie.

After walking past a small group doing *tai chi* exercises in unison, with slow-motion balletic movements, I came upon a self-service cafeteria identified by a sign in English as the "Diamond Restaurant". A short distance ahead, the ramp the driver had brought me down on the way from the airport the day before climbed up to the motorway, and the embankment came to an end to be replaced by warehouses and jetties between the pillars holding up the road. I went into the cafeteria, got a spring roll and a cup of tea and sat in a window seat. Two men going by outside, upon seeing I was foreign, stopped and watched me eat for a while as though confronted by an extraordinary spectacle.

When I finished my breakfast I crossed back to the other side of the Bund and, without any idea of where I wanted to go, walked back the way I had come till I turned into a cobbled street I saw by a creek emptying into the Huangpu a little beyond the Peace Hotel. A massive 1930s apartment block with blackened walls, probably once inhabited by foreign millionaires, rose on the other side of the water, as ugly under the grey sky as any Moscow building from the same period. A motorised barge piled high with dirty white sacks inscribed "Great Star Flour Mills" was chugging upstream. A man in a leather jacket standing outside a closed discotheque named New York, New York grinned at me and called out, "Hey American, I love you!" Concluding there was little to see ahead where the creek meandered under a series of low bridges, I decided to go to the Yuyuan Gardens.

By the time I had made my way through narrow streets with pavements cluttered with parked bicycles to Nanjing Road, the first of the Uighur moneychangers I had seen the previous afternoon had already stationed himself in the same doorway. Because he was busy counting a folded bundle of banknotes concealed in one hand he didn't notice me until I had gone by, but was still able to utter "Change money?" in a just audible voice to my receding back.

I strode away without responding and, stopping one of the city's battered taxis, said, "*Yuyuan Shangsha*". We turned left at the first corner and right at the third one after that. Intending to walk back, I tried to memorise our route, but as we kept turning from one road into another, soon realised I wouldn't be able to. I turned my attention instead to the neglected buildings with their signs in Chinese, the bicycles and the articulated trolleybuses that went by, the odd pedestrian in a Mao suit on the crowded pavements, and the people patiently holding up model cruisers and destroyers on corners here and there.

When we stopped a quarter of an hour later on the edge of a square where another policeman on a circular wooden platform was directing the traffic from inside a metal cylinder resembling an oil drum sawn in half, it was beginning to drizzle again. Pointing at the other side of the square, the driver said a few words in Chinese. I paid him and, crossing over under the drops lightly brushing my face, entered the pedestrianised street he had indicated.

Along the pavement on one side there was a large piece of unpaved ground with stalls selling handicrafts and unidentifiable snacks amongst puddles left from earlier rains. The small restaurants and gift shops with curved roofs on the other side that looked no more than a few years old were clearly designed to be reminiscent of the traditional China not in evidence anywhere else in Shanghai, but they weren't particularly convincing. Going through a passage between two of them, I found myself in a courtyard surrounded by similar buildings where a hawker carrying sets of postcards approached me and held up the five fingers of his right hand.

I gave him the five yuan he wanted and received a handful of cards with various views of the city. The cardboard sleeve in which they came had a paragraph on the back in English where the tenses did not match and at times subject and object became confused:

Shanghai is China's biggest commercial city and number one port. Here not only historic Yuyuan Gardens from the time of the Ming dynasty but latest skyscrapers and the giant television tower went past your eyes. You see the famous Bund and Nanjing Road as they are today. Shanghai will love you so much you'll forget to go home.

The historic gardens were in another courtyard adjacent to the one I had wandered into. I bought a ticket and spent some time looking at attractive summerhouses, peaceful koi ponds, giant vases webbed with tiny cracks under their yellowing glazing and weather-beaten stone lions with narrow heads and large eyes, all of which looked infinitely more authentic than the curved-roofed new buildings next door without being any more typical of the city.

When I came out, the young Japanese woman I had seen checking into the Peace Hotel with her chrysanthemum-emblemed passport was standing in front of a shop some distance away. Today her expensive-looking black coat was complemented by an equally expensive-looking long grey scarf, but because she was peering at something that had caught her attention, she failed to see me. I made my way to the nearby square and, boarding another taxi, went to the former French Concession.

* * *

The new stores lining Huaihai Road, known as Avenue Joffre in Concession days, were as full of Western goods as their predecessors of seven decades ago. After dutifully going into one or two of them, I had a rather late lunch in a nondescript café. By the time, relying on nothing more than my sense of direction, I had, after all, managed to walk back to the Bund under the fine drizzle that kept stopping and starting again, it was almost four o'clock. Pretending not to notice a girl in a slit skirt coming towards me, I crossed over to the other side of the road and went up on the embankment by the Huangpu.

There were once again tugs pulling long lines of barges on the water. The group performing *tai chi* were gone, but not a few strollers were about. As a pair of Uighurs went by, one of them whispered, "Change money?" without turning away from his companion.

Before long I was accosted by a man in his thirties who introduced himself as "Robert" and asked me where I was from.

"England," I told him.

"They say Shanghai resembles London. Is that true?"

If the spot we were at resembled any British city, it was Liverpool – the same murky river, the same grey stone buildings, the same air of dilapidation and loss of past glories. "Yes, it's just like London," I declared.

"London: Buckingham Palace, Big Ben, Victoria Station." He smiled with pleasure at having been able to demonstrate the extent of his knowledge. "And most important of all for me, the Tate Gallery, because I'm an artist."

"I see."

"But I have another occupation as well. Would you like me to show you?"

For a second I was afraid he would say he was a qualified masseur and invite me to his studio for a demonstration, but then I saw him fish a sheet of black construction paper folded in two and a small pair of scissors from his pocket.

Taking hold of my chin with a quick "Allow me", he turned my head towards the light from the river, and, looking at my profile, began cutting the construction paper. He was working with such skill that it wasn't long before he was finished. Placing the scissors back in his pocket, he brought out, instead, a credit-card-sized transparent plastic sleeve into which a piece of cardboard was inserted. "There," he said, placing one of the two identical silhouettes he had produced out of the folded sheet on each side of the cardboard divider, "you can keep one and give the other to somebody close to you; 50 yuan each."

I was annoyed with him for demanding 100 yuan for something I hadn't asked for. "I can't afford to take both," I said; "give me just one."

It was obvious Robert wasn't happy with this idea, but feared that if he objected he might lose me altogether. After thinking for a moment, "It doesn't matter," he said in a conciliatory tone; "if you are going to take one you may keep the other as well." And handing me not just one silhouette but also its twin, which he couldn't possibly sell to anybody else, he took the money I gave him and left.

During the time it had taken for all this to happen, twilight had begun to set in. I put my silhouettes in my pocket, went down from the embankment and crossed the road. But on reaching the Peace Hotel, instead of going up to my room, I made for the rooftop terrace.

There was no one around the steep green copper roof. When I went up to the railing bordering the terrace I saw lights had come on by the darkening river and on the Bund. From below rose the sounds of evening traffic. The red flags by Mao's statue and on top of buildings gleamed in the dying light, and above them neons advertising Compaq, Marlboro and Hitachi were flashing.

As I was watching the darkness slowly deepen, I heard an educated voice say "Good evening" behind me and when I turned round I saw the first of my fellow hotel guests to join me in my eyrie was the young Japanese woman. Clearly, she was one of those well-to-do foreigners whose English, acquired at an early age from private tutors, is better than most natives'. Looking at her properly for the first time, I also became aware of two other facts: her beauty and her unhappiness. Like the former, a function of her fine bone structure and flawless skin, the latter was fully palpable, as though it, too, were a physical characteristic.

She had walked up to the railing and was leaning against it. For a moment we stood side by side in silence like a pair of passengers at the prow of a ship heading out into a dark ocean. Then, more as if talking to herself than to me, she said, "My husband was a pilot. Sometimes I would fly in the same plane as him and we would stay at hotels in foreign cities. I loved Rome. Since we got divorced I travel by myself, but I seem to have lost the instinct for it. The places I visit no longer mean as much to me."

I was not surprised by her words. I knew travel was a period when the ordinary rules did not apply and people would reveal to a stranger they met on a journey something they wouldn't disclose to their closest friend, simply because the stranger was a stranger and their judgement regarding the confession they heard didn't really matter. What she was telling me she found disappointing was not the places she visited but life itself. She had got married and divorced, whatever had happened had happened, and in the midst of her wealthy and privileged existence she had become unhappy. Even though letting me know all this might bring her a degree of momentary relief, she knew well enough that there was nothing I could do for her.

But she seemed to be bothered by my silence and, apparently thinking it would be more courteous if she took some interest in me, "Do you travel much?" she asked.

"Not as much as I'd like."

"What do you do?"

"I have a degree in literature; I do the sorts of things that will let me do."

"I wrote a poem recently. Would you like to hear it?"

And before I had a chance to reply, above the desperate, crazy city whose inhabitants tried to sell everything they could think of from elaborate model ships fashioned out of tin to their own bodies, and were willing to embrace communism, capitalism or anything else to be saved, she recited a poem which was slowly revealed to be laden with a craziness of its own. Called "The Cataract", it was quite short and concerned a woman in her early thirties for whom everything had lost its lustre as if the "inner eye" through which she viewed it was clouding over, condemning her to spending the rest of her days in a flat and grey world where nothing would really attract or move her ever again.

It was obvious that the woman standing next to me was describing herself in the poem she wrote, and even if I didn't dare to turn and look at her face, the tremor that had crept into her voice as she delivered the last lines indicated she had begun to cry. There was no point in saying something mindless like "You are lucky if the world is merely flat and grey for you; for some it's downright terrifying". In any case, she clearly had once again drifted away from me and was lost in her own thoughts. Muttering an excuse I knew she wouldn't really hear or be interested in, I slipped away, went downstairs, and, without acknowledging the American-accented doorman's "Goodbye, sir", stepped out into the street.

It was raining more heavily now, but, still too preoccupied with the woman weeping on the terrace above to bother about getting wet, I walked on, looking at the packed trolleybuses and the neons in Chinese characters reflected on the shiny pavements. The policeman directing traffic from inside his white cylinder at the crossroads seemed to have changed, but his movements were the same as his predecessor's. When his shrill whistle sounded above the horns, the cyclists waiting at the lights with their usual bundles flowed past, pedalling hard under the rain.

Number One Shanghai Provisions Company looked even older in the dark than it had in daylight. For a second I felt that if I turned my head I would find myself in Nanjing Road in the days of the International Settlement, with trams and Sikh policemen in turbans and young soldiers who, because they were from Liverpool, the city I had been thinking of by the river earlier, couldn't speak English as well as the Japanese woman. Everything would be charged with the strange attractiveness of the past and become interesting, different, striking. At the same time, I knew it wouldn't happen. Forty years after first coming across its name in a children's comic, I'd got to Shanghai; but to imagine the world was a colourful and exciting place forever waiting to be discovered and we could simply go on travelling, unaffected by the pain of others or our own growing weariness, was an empty dream. The road was strangely quiet: I looked at the heavily-made-up girls seeking a foreigner to practice their English with, the sad-faced young masseurs trying to keep warm in their flimsy jackets, the Uighur moneychangers sheltering in doorways, and realised that the blue lotus I had left between the pages of a book years earlier had long faded.

SAYONARA, SAVKAR-SAN

A lighter rain than would have been expected from the dark clouds above was falling past the window of my fifteenth-storey hotel room and landing on the tall grey buildings, broad avenues and black-and-white-striped pedestrian crossings of Hiroshima. It was the middle of February and in the end I had found my way to Japan as well. I no longer asked myself why I played this game. Having had to change planes at two airports in Asia to get to this city by the Inland Sea, the next day I would leave again and travel across the mountains that formed the spine of the country to Matsue on the east coast where I would once more spend just a single night before heading for Tokyo nearly seven hundred kilometres away. Going from place to place had ceased to be a passion or even a pastime for me and become a mere instinct I seemed unable to control.

I closed the door of my room and went downstairs. My being in Hiroshima had nothing to do with the primitive atom bomb released above the roofs of the city on the morning of 6 August 1945 from the United States Army Air Force B29 Superfortress the *Enola Gay*. I had decided on such an entry point in part because of its proximity to Matsue, a place of much greater interest to me, and in part the chance it offered of seeing a sizeable portion of the country on my way to Tokyo. All the same, like everyone who came here, I, too, of course had to see the Peace Park located at the spot where the bomb fell.

The hotel, which I had chosen simply because I had found it standing next door to Hiroshima Station where the bus from the airport terminated, had automatically given me a one-page city-map-cum-guide when I registered. According to this, there were trams that left for the Peace Park from the other side of the railway. With the attitude traditionally displayed towards the rest of the world by a nation that believed such things existed only in their own country, the map also had instructions in one corner for the benefit of foreigners who might never have encountered a tram before:

1. *Make sure the vehicle is going to your destination.*
2. *Board through the entry door.*
3. *Wait till you reach your stop.*
4. *As you are leaving, give the fare (150 yen) to the conductor or drop it in the box. If you don't have the right coins, use the change machine by the exit.*

Despite these explanations, because the time was approaching half past three and I had no idea when the Peace Museum in the park would be closing, I did not intend to take a tram. Picking up one of the big umbrellas placed on a stand in the lobby for guests to use, I walked out of the building and made for the taxi stand a short distance away.

The door of the navy-blue cab noiselessly swung open as the uniformed and white-gloved driver responded to my approach by touching a button. Afraid of leaving a mark on the even whiter cover stretched tight over the back seat, I perched on the edge and, unable to remember the name of my destination in Japanese, said "The Peace Park please" in English.

"*Piyusu Parku*," repeated the driver and followed it with a word which I knew meant "Yes" but was barked out with all the ferocity of a sergeant calling his charges to attention: "*Hai!*"

The door swung shut again; we left the station area and entered the traffic following the left-hand side of the road, as in Britain. Sitting as far forward as I could in my anxiety to protect the white seat cover which seemed to belong not to the world of the automatic door but a different one where old women smelling faintly of rosewater crocheted doilies, I noticed a further trace from that other world. In a box placed between the two front seats there were mints wrapped in cellophane to give the passengers a refreshing buzz on their brief journey.

We went over a bridge spanning one of the channels of the Ota river whose delta on the Inland Sea split the city into a number of islands (I seemed to remember reading that "Hiroshima" meant "Broad Island"). Veering slightly to the right, we entered a long avenue with a green strip on either side. The seven or eight-storey buildings beyond the green strips that looked like office blocks were featureless apart from a sign in Japanese here and there. In addition to the Hondas, Toyotas and city buses filling up the main part of the road, the narrow lanes between the green strips and the office blocks were occupied by cyclists travelling with one hand on their handlebars while they held up an umbrella against the hardening rain with the other.

"*Piyusu Buruvaru*," explained the driver, waving a spotless white hand from side to side. In the city that had been on the receiving end of the most savage act committed in the history of warfare, we were on our way to the Peace Park via the Peace Boulevard.

As we waited for the lights to change at a crossroads, three trams went by in rapid succession. The first was a modern vehicle whose flat front and back and half-concealed wheels gave it the appearance of a bus on rails. With their large round headlamps, rivet-studded ungainly bodies and ancient pantographs, though, the other two might already have been in service in the days before the atom bomb.

Shortly after leaving the crossroads behind, we went out on a bridge leading over another channel of the Ota to another island. My map indicated that the Peace Park was located at the northern end of this piece of land that narrowed to a sharp point. On the other side of the bridge, the driver took the first turning, travelled as far as the edge of a vast pedestrianised area paved in concrete, and stopped by a row of phone booths. "*Hai!*" he screamed over the rain now drumming on the roof of the taxi, "*Piyusu Parku!*"

Stuffing the change from the note I gave him into my pocket, I flung myself out of the door as soon as it swung open, ran over to a pair of low buildings linked by a passageway supported by rectangular pillars I took to be the Peace Museum, and went in with water dripping off my clothes.

A sign on the opposite wall said the Museum closed at five and, probably as much because there wasn't long to go until then as because of the bad weather, there was no queue at the booking window underneath. I bought a ticket bearing a colour photograph of the museum taken on a sunny day, and joined the handful of exclusively Japanese visitors milling about in the hall on the ground floor in small groups.

Immediately inside the door there were two large models, one showing the city before and the other after the bomb. Both featured the island narrowing to a sharp point and the T-shaped bridge connecting it to the islands on either side, but whilst the first was full of Japanese houses with curved roofs lining tiny alleys, with a taller concrete building thrown in here and there, the second consisted of an endless flat expanse of rubble from which there occasionally stuck out the ruins of some structure that had managed to escape complete annihilation.

According to the explanation in English that accompanied the models, in 1945 the spot now occupied by the Peace Park had been almost at Hiroshima's exact centre and functioned as its principal shopping and entertainment quarter. The Americans had chosen Hiroshima as their target for not only housing a major garrison but also having a number of geographical features that "created suitable conditions for bombing", and to gauge the impact of their new weapon better they had refrained from making any earlier air raids on the city. Expecting to be bombed sooner or later, however, the municipal authorities had decided to widen some of the alleyways at the centre into firebreaks by having the buildings along them demolished. This was why a substantial portion of the victims of the atom bomb consisted of civilians working on the demolition teams.

Apart from the models, the somewhat dimly lit hall only contained black-and-white photographs hanging on the walls. The first of these, dating from the nineteenth century, showed a group of unsmiling young men whose severely cut uniforms and erect postures suggested they were officer cadets, although it was stated below that they were students. After being an important military centre for centuries, Hiroshima had acquired a modern secondary school during the drive for westernisation under Emperor Meiji, thus becoming an important educational centre as well.

In the captions to the photographs that followed, the nationalist and militarist policies of the 1920s and 30s that had culminated in Japan's invasion of China were treated with a frankness remarkable for a nation not often ready to acknowledge its misdeeds. A scene from a torchlight parade where, unlike the glum students from the Meiji Era, everyone wore a joyful expression carried the comment that even as the taking of the Chinese capital Nanking was being celebrated in

Hiroshima, Japanese soldiers were engaged in slaughtering the inhabitants of the captured city.

I slowly walked past a visual record of the effects on the inhabitants of Hiroshima itself of the subsequent world war, looking at grainy grey images of women receiving military training, teenage girls working in munitions factories, children growing vegetables in their school grounds. Then the photographs ended and a staircase flanked by framed letters of protest written by various mayors of Hiroshima against nuclear tests in different parts of the world took me up to the first floor.

A few technologically minded Japanese were looking at the panels here that explained how nuclear weapons worked, but there was nothing I didn't know in the simplified diagrams showing the splitting of the uranium atom and the emission of gamma rays. The part of the museum that was really about the atom bomb appeared only after I had made my way through the elevated passageway on pillars, filled with the dull sound of the rain outside, to the second building.

In the entrance hall was a circular model, bigger than the ones I had already seen, covering all of Hiroshima, and on the television screens suspended from the ceiling in an even wider circle above, a brief film was playing that showed the *Enola Gay* being loaded with the bomb at an airbase in the Pacific and setting out on its mission. As if to emphasise that, with infinite care and patience, it was bringing a separate death to everyone, the same silver aircraft glinting in the sun rose into the clouds on a dozen different screens and then the film began all over again.

Looking more carefully, I noticed that there was also a bright red sphere hanging over the middle of the model at the end of a transparent cable. It was explained below that this represented the immense fireball that the detonation of the bomb had caused to form above the city. The temperature at the centre of the flames had been in excess of a million degrees, and those on the ground had thought the sun had fallen out of the sky.

A life-size model of the bomb on the wall behind, over three metres long and still looking squat as a result of its huge girth, completed the display. But because the sun's falling out of the sky had destroyed nearly everything, the exhibits in the first part of the main hall I walked into next consisted of a handful of items dug out of the ashes a few days later by survivors looking for some trace of their loved ones. Fifty-nine-year-old demolition-team member Kengo Nikawa's pocket watch, stopped forever at 8.15, the time of the explosion, stood in a glass case by itself with its blackened dial. A little further on, a wire dummy in another glass case sported the tattered uniform once worn by fourteen-year-old secondary-school student Nobuko Shoda, and a third glass case contained the satchel and sewing notebook belonging to another demolition-team member, thirteen-year-old Toshika Sekioka. On the open pages of the notebook, which had somehow escaped incineration inside the satchel, were designs for dresses drawn sixty years earlier by the teenager interested in clothes.

The rest of the hall was devoted to the 60,000 individuals who, over the subsequent days and weeks, followed the 80,000 killed instantly in the blast and those who developed various radiation-related illnesses years later. Walking past panels carrying photographs and information concerning the half-dead lying on pavements, doctors trying to dress burns at hospitals and a group of young women taken to the US for treatment in the 1950s, I reached the last glass case occupied by a collection of bird figures fashioned out of coloured paper and an embroidered kimono made for a child.

According to the information supplied, these were connected with Sadako Sasaki, who had survived the bomb as a two-year-old only to contract leukaemia a decade later due to the after-effects of radiation. Throughout the time she was in hospital she had gone about in her beloved little kimono and, in accordance with Japanese beliefs, tried to make a thousand cranes out of paper to regain her health, but she had died while still short of this target. Now children from all over the world sent paper cranes to be placed at the Sasaki Monument in the Peace Park.

It was hard to decide what to make of all this. The sentimentality displayed towards the victims of the atom bomb elsewhere in the room seemed to reach a peak here. But perhaps that was inevitable; perhaps the ultimate indignity visited on us by death was the way we always ended up becoming the focus of adjectives like "little" and "beloved" and "poor" so that each of us had their tragedy transformed into a meaningless farce.

Feeling oppressed, I walked out of the hall and made my way down several flights of stairs sandwiched between photographs of a series of statesmen ranging from Mikhail Gorbachev to Shimon Peres who had visited Hiroshima in recent years to act out their own brand of farce with solemn faces, till I found a door to let me out into the park behind the museum.

As it was now after half past four, daylight was slowly fading. Although the rain still pouring from the sky indicated drought was not a serious problem in the city, the grass on the ground, perhaps because it had drowned as a result of too much water, was a sickly yellow rather than deep green as in the photograph on my ticket. I stepped out onto the wet concrete strip in the middle reflecting the dim lights of the museum, and walked towards the low arch of the Memorial Cenotaph.

The strip ended at the cenotaph itself containing the names of all those killed by the bomb, and through the curve described by the main part of the Memorial over this, a flame could be seen still flickering under the rain on a concrete block in the middle of the pool on the other side. A plaque stated that the flame would burn not forever but only until the last nuclear device in the world was destroyed. Everything was ready for a cheap joke: *What is optimism? Believing that the flame in the Peace Park will burn not forever but only until the last nuclear device in the world is destroyed.*

Looking at the leafless cherry trees on either side, I tried to imagine the crowds assembled here every year on 6 August to mark another anniversary of the bomb, the speeches made for peace, the fluttering as hundreds of white doves were released to soar into the air, but I failed. Amidst the din of the rain battering the large umbrella above my head with the name of my hotel on it, and the dead yellow grass everywhere, it felt as if the end of the world had come.

Passing by the paper cranes lying wet and crushed at the foot of the Sasaki Monument, I reached the bridge at the tip of the island. Amongst the office blocks and hotels of modern Hiroshima on the edge of the neighbouring island, there rose the dark skeleton of the old Exhibition Hall which, being directly below the bomb's explosion point in mid-air, had been relatively unaffected by the blast waves travelling outwards, and was now preserved as another monument. For a moment I stood there, looking at the exposed girders of the dome resembling a broken skull and the gaping glassless windows resembling eye sockets. Then I walked across the bridge forming a path from the city's past to its present.

The sky was drained of all colour now, and there were lights here and there in the new buildings. I briefly followed the bank of the Ota before turning inland to enter a pedestrianised street transformed into an indoor shopping centre by the canvas canopy placed above its entire length to protect it from the Hiroshima rains.

Yellow lights, necessitated as much by the canopy as by the deepening dark, burned in the florists and shoe shops and amusement arcades on the two sides, and the footsteps and murmurs of shoppers, most of them born years after the atom bomb, echoed in the enclosed space.

Even though, wanting to keep out of the rain for as long as possible, I kept my pace slow, after about two hundred metres I was forced to come out from under the canvas canopy when the street opened up into a broad road. However, I could see that, beyond the pedestrians filling the pavements and the buses and trams caught in the dense evening traffic, the covered shopping zone began again on the other side.

I walked equally slowly in this longer second part and managed to kill some more time in an antiques shop whose scratched and dented metal shelves held nothing more than radios with missing buttons, naked pink plastic dolls, mirrors that had lost their reflective backing in places, and a handful of battered paperback *Kriminalromane* left behind by German tourists.

By the time I reached a second broad road at the end of the covered street, it had grown completely dark and enough neon signs had been switched on to prove that Japan surpassed even the United States in this area. Everywhere red, blue, green, white lights glowed against the dark sky. But the thoroughfare was so wide that the tram stop in the middle still remained beyond the full reach of the rays from either side and couldn't be easily made out.

Shortly after I crossed over and began waiting, one of the lumbering old trams with large round headlamps appeared. Spotting the words "Hiroshima Station" spelt out in English as well as Japanese on the illuminated sign in front of it, I got on, found myself a seat amongst commuters returning from work, and soon reached the station area.

Because nothing had passed my lips for hours I was hungry. In a small eatery a man was seated at the counter behind the window. As he deftly moved his chopsticks back and forth between his mouth and a deep bowl, his gaze stayed glued to the book lying open beside him, identifiable even from outside as a *manga* comic with the usual cast of round-eyed non-Japanese-looking characters engaged in grotesque acts of violence against each other. I went in and had some food myself before making my way to the other side of the station through a large subway with concrete pillars casting long shadows that would have made me wary had I been in any other country than safe, orderly Japan, where I knew random violence to be confined mainly to comic books. Within minutes I had reached my hotel and was back in my room.

As I was on the fifteenth floor, there was no need to draw the curtains. I connected the electric kettle placed on the dresser to Japan's strange 100-volt power supply to make myself tea, watched the news on the only television channel in English I could find, took a shower and, feeling tired after my long day, went to bed before it was quite ten o'clock.

When I woke up at one point in the night the rain had stopped. Most buildings lay in darkness, but here and there a red or blue neon continued to shine, and along empty thoroughfares the streetlamps burned in silent rows. The deserted city seemed to be waiting without a sound for something terrible such as the sun once again falling out of the sky.

* * *

Next morning the English-language *Daily Yomiuri* I picked up at the station forecast more rain, and in places even snow, for the entire country, but it was still dry in Hiroshima. They had explained to me that, to get to Matsue, I'd have to change trains at Okayama one hundred and fifty kilometres to the north, and enclosed two reservation cards with my carriage and seat numbers on them in the envelope containing my ticket. I took a look at the large electronic board above my head to see where the first of my trains would be leaving from, waved my envelope at the official at the barrier and went through.

It seemed that the British technical advisors who were summoned in the last quarter of the nineteenth century to help with Japan's transition to the railway age had taken care to reproduce here the peculiar platforms of their own country, distinguished from those everywhere else by being three times as high. Apart from that, though, there were no similarities between travelling by train in Japan and using the decaying railway system of the United Kingdom. On the envelope containing my reservation cards there was a drawing of one of the ultramodern trains transformed into a symbol of Japanese technology by their ability to travel at speeds ranging from one to three hundred kilometres an hour that were dubbed "Bullet Train" by Westerners, although the Japanese themselves preferred the more modest designation *Shinkansen* (New Mainline Train). As Okayama was on the line to Tokyo, I would complete the first stage of my journey in one of these vehicles resembling a wingless jet with their round nose and aerodynamic body.

Along the edge of the high platform there were numbers to indicate where each carriage would be stopping. I was used to trains arriving and departing punctually in this corner of Asia, but clearly in Japan the process had been taken one stage further and the precise point of departure could be guaranteed as well. There were already passengers waiting in a queue at each number, but as another train would be leaving from the same platform before mine, these queues had nothing to do with me. I only glanced at them briefly before beginning to walk up and down in the background with my small holdall.

Because everything looked new and clean, and the Japanese preference for saving over spending meant that there was very little advertising about compared to America or Europe, the station had a curiously unfinished air. When an aluminium-bodied local train turned up a few minutes later and took away everyone in the queues, leaving the platform half-empty, this impression became even stronger. Then another aluminium-bodied train picked up those waiting on one of the opposite platforms, and it was followed by a gleaming white *shinkansen*, identical to the drawing on my reservation card, that swept in like a descending Boeing and left again exactly twenty-five seconds later.

My own *shinkansen* that arrived at sixteen minutes past nine o'clock was an even more advanced model with a still closer resemblance to an aeronautical creation. I settled into my seat at the very front of the second carriage and looked at a sign that said laptops could be plugged into a socket on the floor. The other passengers, who seemed mostly to be businessmen, had, in quite a few cases, taken off their jackets and loosened their ties because of the warmth inside and were at work at their computers, putting the finishing touches to the presentations they would be making in Tokyo. By the time I registered all this, the train, not only incredibly fast but incredibly silent as well, was already underway.

A musical gong was followed by a woman's voice that thanked us first in Japanese and then in English for travelling with Japanese Railways and stated Okayama would be our first stop. Gathering speed, we began passing through tunnels carved into the hills surrounding Hiroshima.

In the green valleys between the hills, villages consisting of Japanese houses with curved roofs stood under the grey sky, and here and there a larger town could be seen amongst the rice paddies. For a brief moment we travelled alongside a stream, and at another point passed by a small, still lake.

I knew that these glimpses of rural life and nature didn't really reflect the realities of contemporary Japan where, out of a population of one hundred and fifty million, twenty-five million lived in and around Tokyo, and most of the rest were crammed into a handful of cities on the east coast. For the time being, though, I had no objection to spending some time in this other Japan which, if atypical, was also more attractive.

The unpretentious small green train I switched to at Okayama, where the *shinkansen*, having swallowed up one hundred and fifty kilometres in less than forty minutes, dropped me shortly before ten, seemed to belong to the same atypical world. My carriage, even warmer than the one on the *shinkansen*, but also narrower and shorter, had no occupants other than a teenager listening to his Walkman, two young women talking quietly among themselves and an elderly couple who looked as if they were on their way to visit their grandchildren. Once again, we left exactly on time and, after making our way through the city's suburbs at a stately pace more appropriate for a train, turned towards the Chukogu Mountains on the horizon.

The hills on either side were covered in pines, cedars and evergreen Japanese *kashi* oaks. The river Takashi foamed and rushed between these, occasionally staying beside the railway for a while before moving away to avoid a hill pierced by a tunnel, keeping out of sight on the other side and then suddenly reappearing below as we crossed a bridge.

The curved-roofed settlements on the hills now looked even more rural. As a testimony to the propensity of the Shinto religion to turn a pond or a tree or a rock into a god, a small temple stood here and there, entered through a *torii* consisting of two posts topped by a pair of lintels that symbolised the transition from the profane to the sacred world. Because Shinto considered the dead as gods as well, graves had not been collected into large cemeteries as in other parts of the world, but placed in groups of five or six in small plots among the houses some of which had their own *torii*. From time to time a more substantial temple dedicated to Buddhism, the second religion of most Japanese along with Shinto, also went past the windows with its red lanterns and stone statues.

As we climbed higher up into the mountains and the temperature fell, the heat in the carriage became less noticeable. When I raised my head at one point, I spotted a sprinkling of snow on top of the highest line of trees. The snow gradually descended to the lower branches, then to the lower trees and finally to the ground. The small stations the train rattled through with a short whistle blast now lay under a thick white blanket, dazzling enough to suggest a recent top-up. Finally, the predicted fresh fall began: large flakes were slowly drifting from the sky as we arrived at Nimni, the halfway point on our journey.

After we dropped the teenager with the Walkman and the two young women off at this medium-sized town and got going again, I left the elderly couple by themselves and went out into the area at the end of the carriage to take a closer look at the snow. The flakes had grown even larger and resembled not so much real flakes as a child's drawing of them. But after continuing at this rate for five or ten minutes, the snow got lighter and before long stopped altogether. We went on travelling across this latest puffy layer of whiteness.

In a village we entered a few minutes later, a man was clearing away the snow in front of his door while a woman, who had put on a black coat that looked as if it belonged to somebody else over a faded red kimono, walked past, her gait rendered awkward as much by the wooden clogs on her feet as by the snowy pavement. Then we reached the end of the village and I saw an old lorry crossing a steel bridge over the Takahashi. On Christmas-time journeys in America thirty years earlier, drunk on a combination of the feeling of freedom brought about by being on holiday, the books I dreamed of writing, and the country itself, which, although I had little affection for it, could always move me with its vastness, I had stared in much the same way out of train windows at the snow-covered plains of the Midwest. I still kept going on journeys, but America had shrunk to Japan and I was now travelling not with passion and conviction but only because travelling had become a habit. Maybe that was what lay behind the hollow feeling I had from time to time that everything had changed and grown old.

The lorry had dropped behind. I returned to the main part of the carriage, sat down at random in one of the seats, nearly all of which now belonged to me, and, wiping away the film of condensation that had formed on the inside of the window, continued to look out.

Because we had started making our way down from the mountains, the snow was now withdrawing. At first the layer on which we were travelling got flatter and thinner, and then increasingly large pieces of ground began to show through. But white patches never fully disappeared: they were still there in places when we reached Yonago on the west coast an hour later.

The Sea of Japan, which I had last seen glinting under the sun two years earlier in Korea, was grey and choppy. After leaving Yonago, we followed the shore for a while, before turning slightly inland and travelling for another twenty minutes until we reached Matsue located between two small lakes linked to each other by a short river and connected to the sea at one end.

The giant storage tanks and the long lines of tanker wagons we passed as we arrived at the station suggested that the city's traditional economic pursuit, fishing, was now supplemented by activities connected with the chemicals industry. Leaving the elderly couple to put on their thick coats and scarves, I got out, walked along a platform with a few bits of snow here and there, and made my way down a set of steps to the exit.

The square in front of the station was cold and deserted. In the depths of winter I had come to a place few people outside Japan had even heard of, and I had no idea where I would be spending the night. For a moment I stood on the pavement, looking about me, until I saw a white modern building ahead that had the word "Hotel" inscribed on it in Latin characters.

"Are you here on business?" asked the man in glasses at Reception as he was checking me in.

For a crazy moment I thought of telling him I worked as a chemical engineer for a company in Birmingham and had come to Matsue to purchase nitrogen and acetone. I was married, with two children. My daughter was about to go to university and, yes, she wanted to study Japanese Literature. As contradicting others wasn't a Japanese habit, the receptionist would probably say nothing even if nitrogen and acetone weren't substances that could be obtained here. But in the end I pulled myself together and answered his question in the negative.

"Business is the only reason most people come here," he said, smiling shyly as though apologising for the city.

"There is something special I want to see."

At this point even an Englishman might have been unable to prevent himself from asking what that was, but the person I was speaking to had received an upbringing that forbade such curiosity. He contented himself with bending his head and completing the check-in procedure.

Because there was little point in going up to take a look at a room where I was going to spend only a single night, I turned down the key he held out to me, and, saying I would be back later, left my holdall with him and walked out again.

Immediately outside the station I had noticed a long hut with a sign that said "Information" in English. Despite this, the woman I found tidying the counter when I walked in seemed to speak only Japanese. Hearing me mention my sole reason for being in Matsue, though, she understood and, scribbling a number and a few words on a piece of paper, gave it to me.

From her pointing at the bus stand at the other end of the square as she did so, I gathered that if I got on the bus with that number and showed the sentence she had written to the driver, I would be let off where I wanted to go. But when the bus, whose schedule I didn't know, failed to turn up after I had been waiting for nearly ten minutes, I walked off and had lunch in a jazz café with piped music and black-and-white photographs of Miles Davis and Billie Holiday, operated in a nearby street by a group of young people determined to prove there was life on the country's sparsely populated west coast as well. By the time I returned to the stand and boarded my bus, it was almost half past two.

We went down a road with fishmongers, car repair shops and a Buddhist temple with snow on its curved roof before crossing a bridge over the river linking the two lakes. Provincial streets with squat buildings of a few storeys followed, but a few minutes later we entered a much more striking area.

Carefully restored traditional Japanese houses lined one side of the road while on the other was a broad canal on the opposite bank of which stood a steep hill covered in trees that came all the way down to the edge of the water. I knew that the canal was in fact a moat that turned the hill into an island, and somewhere amongst the trees on the peak was Matsue Castle. During the centuries when the powerful Tokugawa family had ruled the country through a series of puppet emperors, the Castle had always been occupied by a feudal lord loyal to the Tokugawas. In the houses by the road, meanwhile, there had lived samurai loyal to the lord, and the system had lasted until the Tokugawas had been ousted by the westernising Emperor Meiji.

The place I was looking for had nothing to do with the Castle or the samurai houses, but because I knew it, too, was along this road, I got ready to get off. At a junction where the road opened up into another narrow provincial street and the moat veered off to the left, the driver stopped the bus and, turning towards me, uttered a few words in Japanese. Glancing out of the window on the right I recognised the house with the curved roof that looked smaller than it did in photographs. Then I got out through the door on the other side of the vehicle and saw the grey bust standing on a stone pedestal by a snow-covered bench facing the water.

The man it depicted was around my age, but the white streaks the snow had added to the hair of the bust made him look older. Although he was a Westerner, because of the way he screwed up and narrowed his eyes, one of which had been injured in a childhood accident, he could almost have been taken for Japanese. Conscious of our finally having met, I stood there for a moment, looking at him.

I had managed to get hold of and read only a tiny portion of the writings of Lafcadio Hearn whose name I had first come across in an anthology years earlier, but I knew his life story by heart. He was born in 1850 on the Ionian island of Lefkas of a Greek mother and an Irish father who was a surgeon with the British Army, and his unusual forename "Lafcadio" in fact meant "of Lefkas".

His father's posting to the West Indies when Hearn was two had led to the child's being sent to Dublin together with his mother. But, unable to get used to either the climate or the mores of Ireland, she had soon abandoned him to return to Greece, and he had been brought up by an aunt of his father's and educated at a succession of schools first in Dublin and then in France and England.

The decline of his great-aunt's financial circumstances had forced him to emigrate to the United States in 1869 and he had worked as a journalist in Ohio until being fired as a result of the scandal caused by his marrying a black woman. The marriage had collapsed soon afterwards and Hearn had moved once again, this time to French-controlled Martinique.

Translations from French, which he spoke fluently, and a number of travel books on Martinique and other Caribbean locations had brought him a degree of literary fame, prompting an American magazine to offer him a temporary assignment in Japan. Taking advantage of the Meiji reforms then in progress, he had stayed in the country after the expiry of his magazine contract, finding a job as an English teacher at the new high school in Matsue, marrying the daughter of a local samurai family and assuming Japanese citizenship and the name Koizumi Yakumo. His fame had grown considerably with the stories and articles on Japanese life he had begun to write after this point and he had gone on to become a professor of literature in Tokyo, dying there of a heart attack in 1904 without ever returning to Europe.

All this had flooded into my mind once again as I stood by the side of the road where the bus had dropped me off. I lifted my head to take another look at the face of the man who had interested me sufficiently to make me come to Matsue, then I crossed over and walked into his restored house.

In the small entrance hall hung a poster showing the colourful doors of Dublin's Georgian town houses which I was accustomed to seeing in tourist information centres and travel agencies all over the British Isles, but which seemed out of place at this remote spot. Under the poster, an attractive girl was sitting at a table that had information leaflets about Hearn on it, although the neat stacks in which they stood indicated no visitor had yet braved the cold to turn up and handle them today. I took one and, passing by a large glass case containing the high writing desk specially designed to help the author overcome the problems with his vision, went through to the low-ceilinged Japanese room next door.

A video screen was embedded in the wall by the entrance with a row of buttons under it. When I pressed the one marked "English", the screen came to life and a woman's voice with a faint Irish accent said, "This is the story of a man wandering the world. Hearn's first name comes from 'Lefkas', the island where he was born, while his last is ultimately derived from the German verb *irren* meaning 'wander', 'stray' or 'err'."

The video went on to divide Hearn's life into five periods labelled as "Greece", "Western Europe", "The United States", "The Caribbean" and "Japan", showed his "footprints" on a map of the world, and concluded with the information that there was now a car park named after him in Martinique.

Because, like most people who keep going from place to place, Hearn had accumulated little in the way of worldly goods, there wasn't a great deal to see in the glass cases around the room. A selection of his books, most of them published in Japan, was accompanied by one or two letters he had written, the iron dumbbells he had exercised with while living in Matsue, and the large conch he had enjoyed blowing like a horn. Next to these were the cage of the nightingale given to him by a friend as a present during an illness, the purple sash used, Japanese-style, as a sling to carry his books in during his Tokyo days, and an old newspaper with a set of simple sentences penned on it in two-inch-high letters in a bid to teach his son English: "I DRINK, YOU DRINK, HE DRINKS. I RUN, YOU RUN, HE RUNS."

When I turned to the glass case along the opposite wall, I saw an ink "portrait" of Hearn made as he was about to sail from New York to Japan. But, instead of showing his face the way a normal portrait would, it showed the back of his head and shoulders as, dressed in a suit and a broad-brimmed hat, he performed his characteristic action of walking away from everything which until recently had made up his existence. And below was a chair with the suit and the hat depicted in the drawing draped over it as if their owner had finally walked away from them as well.

I left the room, passed by the girl still sitting with her information leaflets and went out. The objects I had seen, though few in number, were sufficient to conjure up the strangeness of a life which had begun with the acquiring of a name suggestive of wandering, and was now commemorated by a car park built to enable others to wander. Hearn had perhaps deliberately conjugated the wrong verbs on his newspaper dated 1895. The real verbs that governed his life were different: "I AM WANDERING, ALWAYS WANDERING, CEASELESSLY WANDERING. I AM GOING, ALWAYS GOING, CEASELESSLY GOING."

Ignoring the cold that seemed to have got worse, I thrust my hands into my pockets, followed the curve of the moat and crossed by an old stone bridge to the island where the castle stood. Because the weather had kept visitors away not just from Hearn's house but here as well, there was more snow around than in other parts of the city. In the garden of the temple at the foot of an asphalt path that made its way up among the trees stood an evergreen *kashi* with a piece of rope tied round its trunk to show it was holy. There were also rows of wooden prayer tablets hanging from the railings outside, but as the words written on them were in Japanese, I couldn't make out what was being prayed for.

Listening to the snow crunch under my feet, I climbed up the path to a clearing at the peak surrounded by *kashis* and pines. Unlike its counterparts in Europe and the Middle East, the castle that occupied one end was not a structure with towers and crenellations and arrow slits but merely a large Japanese house of a few storeys with a curved roof. Perhaps because it was winter, its wooden door was firmly shut. From the pole outside drooped an absolutely motionless white Japanese flag, the disc at its centre representing the sun visible only as a red streak amongst the folds.

I walked over to the other side of the clearing where the path started descending again, and looked down. It was the last hour of the day before the lights come on, and the modern buildings of Matsue below appeared dazzlingly white in the deepening gloom. I then looked out towards the spot in the distance where the larger of the city's two lakes opened up to the sea. Hearn must have often stood there at sunset, eyeing the wooden houses and the reeds and the fishing boats with the keen interest the rootless take in everything around them. At such times, had he tried to convince himself that this was home and he was Japanese, even as memories of other countries and lives he had known formed and tumbled in his head, telling him he was only a wanderer, a fraud, an identity thief?

The sky appeared a little more luminous over the sea, but I couldn't possibly make it to the shore before evening fell, and I didn't really want to go anywhere else that day. In the silence of the clearing a bird let out a long, low cry somewhere, complaining of the cold and the approaching dark.

Deciding not to stay any longer, I began making my way down the snowy path.

★ ★ ★

The next day I passed through the same snow-blanketed villages in the same small train and got on another *shinkansen* at Okayama as noon was coming. This time, though, we didn't leave Okayama. Despite the speed of the *shinkansen*, half an hour after our departure we were not in open country but in suburbs composed of four or five-storey apartment and office blocks interspersed with factories and warehouses. Occasionally a small snow-patched field or a bit of empty space appeared, but before long the buildings began again and everywhere pylons taller than the buildings marched off towards the grey mountains that stayed permanently on the horizon to the west.

After another half hour, with Okayama seemingly still not finished, a musical chime ushered in the announcement that we were arriving at Kobe, and following our brief stop there, the office blocks and factories and pylons began again. The size of the population had forced the cities squeezed into the strip between the mountains and the sea to grow towards each other and merge, with the result that what looked like separate places on the map were in fact all part of the same vast conurbation stretching for hundreds of kilometres. Apart from the buildings growing taller and the factories and the pylons briefly disappearing whenever we reached a city centre, the view didn't change. By Osaka I had started losing interest and by Yagoda was glancing out of the window only occasionally. But as we were approaching Tokyo towards four in the afternoon, the buildings got truly tall, the roads became bigger, and as the coastal strip widened at this point, the mountains vanished, allowing the city to stretch in all directions. As soon as the *shinkansen* had come to a halt amongst all this as though it was touching down on a runaway, I grabbed my holdall and hastened out of the carriage with a feeling of liberation born of having finally arrived somewhere a bit different.

Because the evening rush hour had not quite started, the maze of passages under Tokyo Station still contained only fast-flowing ordinary daytime crowds, instead of being choked with barely moving walls of pedestrians. Taking advantage of the fact that the illuminated signs above were in English as well as Japanese, I found out the direction I had to go in and began walking.

All the sources I had consulted were agreed that Tokyo was not so much a single city with a definite "centre" as a collection of separate districts each of which was almost a mini city in itself. Of these districts, I had chosen Ikebukuro half an hour from Tokyo Station, and booked myself into a relatively inexpensive hotel aimed at Japanese businessmen rather than foreign tourists. My plan was to stay there and travel around the city on the circular Yamanote Line used every day by thousands of commuters.

I found the booking window I was looking for, bought my ticket and returned to the upper level. I had seen very little snow on the ground as the *shinkansen* arrived in Tokyo, but there was a faint white area at either end of the platform and it felt cold enough for a fresh fall to begin at any moment. Japanese wrapped up in thick coats and parkas stood waiting with their breath misting in the icy air.

When the train arrived, though, it was, as usual, too warm inside for a coat. There were empty seats, but both because I had spent the greater part of the day sitting and because I was afraid of missing my stop, I remained standing and compared the names of the stations we called at with the map above the door all the way to Ikebukuro.

It was beginning to get dark and there were lights in the department stores, sandwich shops and cafés round the square outside the station. Neons shone here and there in the two broad thoroughfares leading off the other side, and although not many vehicles were about, from somewhere there drifted the sound of horns heralding the start of the evening traffic.

The lights were on also in my hotel located a few hundred metres down the thoroughfare on the right, and they did little to disguise the smallness of the lobby. To prevent queues forming in such a confined area, the management seemed to have completed all the registration forms in advance, using the information supplied by the guests at the time of booking. When I identified myself, the young man at Reception immediately printed mine off, and as soon as I had signed it, I had my door card.

Like the lobby, the lift, too, felt cramped; but my room on the tenth floor was big enough to make it possible to forget I was in Tokyo where property prices and rents were exorbitant and most people had only a tiny space to live in. From the picture window extending from one end to the other of one wall, the endless apartment and office blocks of the sprawling city could be seen, with most of their windows lit up now, while in the background the white peak of Mount Fuji rose against a sky which had not yet completely lost its greyness.

When I checked the nightstand by the king-size bed, in the drawer which holds a Bible in hotel rooms in the English-speaking world I found a bilingual volume in English and Japanese called *The Teaching of Buddha* and, as I would normally have done with the Bible, opened it and read a passage at random:

Oh my mind! Why do you hover so restlessly over the changing circumstances of life? Why do you make me so confused and restless?

Why do you urge me to collect so many things? You are like a plough that breaks into pieces before it enters the field; you are like a rudder that is dismantled before it sets out on the sea of life and death.

In the same drawer lay a heavy torch sheathed in yellow plastic. It wasn't easy to determine whether this was a precaution against the "Big Shake" that Tokyo, positioned as it was on one of the world's major fault lines, would experience sooner or later, or against the "Big Dark" that was equally inevitable in a country that overheated all its public vehicles and placed neons everywhere even as its nuclear power stations kept being found unsafe and closed down, weakening the national grid further by the day. I pushed the button on the torch and played its powerful beam on the pillows to confirm it worked before returning it to its place by the book.

On top of the TV set positioned in the corner formed by the picture window and the wall facing the foot of the bed was a long and narrow colour brochure printed on cardboard thick enough for it to stand up by itself. The girl on the cover, whose sleeveless blouse hung from her shoulders on straps no thicker than shoestrings, wasn't as round-eyed as a *manga* heroine, but as her eyes weren't quite narrow either, it was obvious she had been chosen because she didn't look Japanese. Inside the brochure it was explained that, in addition to four free television channels, there was an "Adult Channel" that offered paid viewing. Those not content with the enlightenment provided by Buddha would be able to use this facility to watch such films as *The Story of the Breasts*, *The Shameless Mouth* and *The Boss and His Secretary*.

As the room was going to be my temporary home for the next three nights I placed the few items in my holdall where I wanted them. I then put on a second pullover against the cold, took the tiny lift back to the ground floor and went out.

It was now fully dark and the sky had finally exchanged its daytime grey for the deep blue of evening. The cast-iron posts by the kerb held up large octagonal lamps that looked as though they had started off as gas-lighting in the Meiji era. The traffic was dense, with a line of white headlamps crawling up one lane and a line of red taillights crawling down the other. Looking at the offices with their signs in Japanese on the upper floors of the blocks on either side and the fishmongers and banks and bookshops at street level, I walked along.

Shortly after I had passed a restaurant in the process of opening up for the night, a crow settled noisily on a pine on the edge of the pavement. With its sleek black plumage and its large, well-fed body that rendered it entirely unlike the skinny Asian crows I had seen in Kuala Lumpur, it looked fit and utterly fearless. I had heard of these notorious birds which had invaded the city and were accused of everything from carrying off baby animals to attacking children and even grown-ups in parks and other open spaces. It was said that, ironically, the problem was caused by the cleanliness of the Japanese, with frequent rubbish collections providing a steady supply of bags outside houses which the crows could tear open to look for food. Why no one had thought of placing domestic waste in the sort of peck-proof bags used in English seaside towns against gulls was not clear.

The road had started descending at a gentle angle. In narrow side streets there now stood one or two-storey white pre-Meiji Japanese houses, the light streaming from behind their curtains falling on the lovingly pruned shrubs in their gardens. I then spotted a temple with a curved roof a little further ahead that had a row of paper lanterns burning outside. Next door was a graveyard shoehorned into the world of the living in the traditional way. Because of the height of the fence outside, only the tops of the tombstones could be made out; but the slope of the ground meant that the entrance to the neighbouring office block was reached by a set of steps, and between this entrance and the main door of the building, positioned some way back from the road, was a passage the right-hand side of which consisted of only a waist-high wall, with the space above it left empty as though the architect had wanted the graveyard to be visible as a *memento mori*. I went up the steps and, leaning against the wall, looked down.

Although much larger than the burial places I had seen on the way to Matsue, the plot still contained only about a hundred graves. Because the tombstones, standing close to one another with snow between and on them here and there, weren't the slabs of western graveyards but tall and thin rectangular prisms, they looked like a model of a city composed of skyscrapers. A few had an even taller piece of wood with writing on it stuck in the ground beside them. As wood was a material that would decay over time, these additions couldn't have been meant as a permanent part of the graves and had to be prayer boards instead. I knew Lafcadio Hearn, too, was buried in a cemetery in Ikebukuro, but because of the habit of placing the dead in small groups in any available space amongst the houses, I wasn't sure if this was that cemetery.

I went down the steps again and kept walking. At a crossroads I reached shortly, roadworks affecting traffic lights were in progress and the vehicles were being directed by a policeman whose white helmet gleamed in the dark. After hesitating for a moment, I decided to stay on the same road and crossed over when the policeman blew his whistle.

Immediately on the other side there was a line of hotels followed by more office blocks. Looking at the commuters returning from work, the shoppers coming out of minimarkets and the crows settling in trees for the night, I pressed on. Although I had been walking for more than half an hour since leaving my hotel, it didn't look as if the road would be ending soon. With a breeze coming from the opposite direction, my face felt frozen and was beginning to hurt. At least to have the breeze on my back, I crossed to the other side of the road and began going back the way I had come. But before long I spotted what appeared to be a branch of an American-style restaurant chain called Jonathan's and went in to get out of the cold.

Because it was early, there were hardly any diners inside. A diminutive young waitress who had a green apron over her white uniform led me to a table by the window, chattering all the while in Japanese despite my obvious inability to understand a single word. I asked for a chicken sandwich and tea by pointing to the illustrations in the laminated menu she held open for me, waited for her to leave with my order and began to rub my hands together to restore the circulation in them.

True to American traditions, the sandwich that eventually arrived was accompanied by a small mound of mixed salad and a helping of chips. I popped a chip in my mouth, took a sip from my tea and, realising I wasn't only cold but hungry as well, began eating with greater determination. When, with the edge of my hunger blunted, I stopped for a rest a few minutes afterwards, I was surprised to discover that the warmth I had received from the food was accompanied by an unaccustomed sense of wellbeing. I had arrived in Tokyo and once more become part of the life of a big city. I had a place to stay, food to eat, and time to look at my surroundings. What more could a traveller want?

By the time I left the restaurant it was coming up to seven o'clock. The sky had changed to black, with a sickle moon hanging in one corner of it and, as a result of those still returning from work being joined by those who had returned earlier and had now come out again in search of entertainment, the pavements were crowded. When I reached my hotel I went on walking towards the station, but, instead of sticking to the road, took to the side streets.

The nightlife area of Ikebukuro seemed to start here. Along narrow thoroughfares stood small clubs and bars the glow from whose neon signs mingled with the rays from the coloured bulbs around their doors. Interspersed with these were equally small restaurants displaying amazingly realistic plastic models of the dishes they served, and karaoke establishments whose barkers for some reason all seemed to be young women in identical red raincoats.

After making my way through half a dozen such streets, on a corner across from the station I came upon my first *pachinko* parlour. Those successful in this game involving guiding tiny steel balls cascading inside a special machine into the appropriate holes below won a token prize such as a packet of paper handkerchiefs or a bar of chocolate. I remembered watching a television documentary according to which one theory for the vast popularity of *pachinko* was that it gave the normally sedate and law-abiding Japanese a chance to experience some of the thrill of betting and taking risks in a country where most forms of gambling were banned. But, apart from failing to explain why *pachinko* was better suited for this purpose than any other game, this struck me as unconvincing in itself. At any rate, the rows of players I could now see staring intently from their seats at the screens in front of them amidst the deafening clatter of steel balls that could be heard outside gave the impression less of savouring forbidden pleasures than of trying to lose themselves in a mechanical task.

When I reached the other end of the long subway under the station I found myself in an even bigger shopping and entertainment area. Eye-catching department stores, restaurants and cinemas lined broad roads, and crowds flowed down the pavements under the neons. Joining them, I, too, spent more than an hour wandering from road to road, looking in shop windows, before the biting cold finally opted for by the weather in place of the expected snow forced me to step into a café and have another tea. By the time I walked back through the subway to the other side of the station, listening to the distant rumble of the Yamanote Line trains above, it was almost half past nine.

Although they had looked as if they would stay open forever, the shops were mostly shut now and Ikebukuro had grown quiet. Looking for signs of life, I entered the maze of narrow streets where the nightclubs were located. But the late hour, the cold and the silence had together destroyed my buoyant mood of earlier on and changed the way I saw my surroundings. I was in a city where people with nowhere else to go killed time in *pachinko* parlours or watched films on the "Adult Channel" in hotel rooms. The world was full of such cities, rooms and people, and I was someone who merely went from place to place, looking at all this.

As if to confirm that I was right, from inside a karaoke bar I was walking past, there rose the drunken voice of a salaryman who had downed half a bottle of Japanese-made Suntory whisky and was now singing "Yesterday". He had said something wrong that had caused the woman he loved to leave him, and he longed for yesterday. Suddenly he wasn't half the man he used to be; there was a shadow hanging over him; yesterday was what he believed in.

Seeing me stop to listen to the lyrics and thinking I was trying to make up my mind to go in, the barker standing by the door in her red raincoat grabbed my arm and said, "Come, you sing, too."

"There aren't any songs I know," I told her.

But, imitating the girl's Japanese accent, "Come, you sing, too," a mocking voice repeated in my ear and went on to list a number of cheap, sentimental but undeniably appropriate songs: *Leaving on a Jet Plane... Take Me Back to Chicago... What Kind of a Fool am I?*

As if the girl hadn't heard me the first time, "There aren't any songs I know" I repeated and, pulling my arm out of her grip, walked down the narrow street with its quietly shining neons.

⋆ ⋆ ⋆

It was past nine when I was awakened by a pair of crows having a dispute over the ownership of one of the roofs across the road. I had perhaps slept so late in an effort to get away from the thoughts in my mind the evening before. But as I didn't want to go anywhere during the morning rush hour that lasted until nearly ten o'clock, I hadn't lost anything. Even after I got dressed and went out I walked at an unhurried pace and managed to delay myself sufficiently to catch an uncrowded train into the city.

Tokyo Station, which I hadn't seen before from the outside, was a brick structure whose close resemblance to the Victorian railway termini of northern Europe suggested it was constructed at the start of the westernisation period. At the bottom of the half-moon-shaped square in front of it began a boulevard flanked by office blocks tall enough to be considered skyscrapers.

When I crossed over and began walking down this thoroughfare I saw similar blocks in the streets on either side. Under the overcast winter sky the buildings looked grey and subdued, and the handful of pedestrians left on the pavements by the ending of the rush hour added to this air of lifelessness with the white surgical masks most of them had donned against the germs they believed they could catch even in this ruthlessly clean country. The only source of vitality and colour seemed to be the yellow, orange and green cabs of different taxi companies that went by from time to time. *My mind, why do you make me collect all these things?*

I headed in the direction indicated by an arrow-shaped sign that had the words "Imperial Plaza" on it in English. A little further on, the boulevard opened up into a multi-lane road where the traffic was heavier. To the left, Tokyo Tower could be seen amongst the skyscrapers in the distance. But, ironically, by acquiring a tower before any other city in the Far East, Tokyo had ended up being left behind in the tower race. The steel structure, built fifty years earlier in imitation of the Eiffel, looked outmoded compared to its space-age counterparts elsewhere in Asia.

I walked across a bridge spanning the moat of the Imperial Palace running along the other side of the road and entered a path between leafless cherry trees with a ring of snow round their base. At the end of the path was a vast, windy square covered in gravel which another sign identified as the Imperial Plaza. Here and there on the gravel lay half-thawed bits of snow resembling tattered rags. Listening to the wind and the distant sound of traffic, I walked on.

At the diagonally opposite corner of the square, where the inner moat surrounding the main palace garden joined with the outer moat, there was a stone bridge with two arches. Behind the high wall at the other end of this stood even higher pines and oaks, hiding the palace from view except for its rooftops. When the Emperor's birthday came, the giant gate the bridge led to would be thrown open for a few hours and thousands of Tokyoans would pass through the gardens, waving small Japanese flags and loudly wishing "*Banzai!*" (ten thousand years) to their sovereign watching them from a room on an upper floor with a bulletproof picture window. Now, though, the gate was shut, and the only souls about apart from me were the two guards in navy-blue uniforms standing outside.

But I'd not come all the way here in vain. When the time reached the hour, a smaller gate within the main one opened, two other guards in navy-blue uniforms came out, marched over to their comrades, swinging their arms in an exaggerated fashion, and, with a shouted exchange, took over the watch. The two previous guards then marched away with the same jerky movements as though they were clockwork toys and stepped inside. The small gate closed after them, and once again silence descended, broken only by the wind and the traffic in the distance.

I turned my back on the palace and walked away across the expanse of gravel with its ragged patches of snow till I left the plaza behind. It took me a few more minutes of walking along the outer moat to reach the gate in the wall surrounding the East Garden which, unlike the main palace garden, was open to the public all year round.

The official sitting in the hut immediately inside the gate handed me a white plastic token with an inscription on it that stated it had to be surrendered on exit. I had come across this security measure in other parts of the world before: if the number of tokens handed out did not match the number returned at the end of the day, it would be assumed someone had decided to stay in the grounds for some illicit purpose.

Obtaining a map of the garden from a second hut a little further on, I discovered that the rules that had to be followed were not restricted to the return of the white token. On the reverse of the sheet it was stated that it was forbidden to hold meetings of a political or any other nature, play games or "make hideous noises" here.

Although the map showed large green areas, the garden was in a curious state of neglect. The lawns by the paths were mostly under snow, but the bits that were exposed were yellow like the lawns in the Peace Park at Hiroshima, the plants in the beds were stunted and ugly, and Tokyo crows had staked their claim to the trees.

Because the garden had two other gates and provided a shortcut to areas neighbouring the palace, there were other people on the paths. As I walked on, I kept coming across ruins of the outposts that had guarded the castle situated in these grounds in the days when the emperors still lived in Japan's old capital Kyoto, and Tokyo was a city called "Edo" belonging to the Tokugawas who were the real power in the land. But it wasn't to look at these that I'd entered the garden: when I shortly reached the large hillock on which the ruins of the castle itself stood, I made my way round it and, surrendering my token, went out through the northern gate.

A concrete bridge led across the outer moat, which, having been drained at this point, was revealed to be impressively deep, and the road beyond had a footbridge over it. I climbed up the steps, crossed over to the other side and walked through a snow-covered park towards Yasukuni, notorious as "the most controversial temple in Japan".

There was almost no one on the broad uphill brick path that began on the other side of the temple's massive *torii* with the height of a four or five-storey building and the appearance of being made of steel. After walking for a few hundred metres, I passed under a second *torii*, this one shown to be of bronze by the green it had oxidised to, and I saw the temple ahead.

The single-storey structure, open at the front, had a simple curved roof. From the gilded eaves hung a white cloth with four large stylised chrysanthemums printed on it in a row. Through the inverted "V" this was pulled up into, the altar could be seen against the far wall, and in the foreground was a low railing and a stone-paved area where worshippers could kneel to pray.

I was a little taken aback by all this. What made Yasukuni controversial was that it was dedicated to Japanese soldiers killed in wars since the Meiji period. Since Shintoism regarded the dead as gods, this meant that members of the armed forces killed in the Second World War were also automatically deified, to the fury of those Japanese believing their country had been the aggressor in that conflict. Nor had matters been helped by successive prime ministers who, disregarding the constitution separating religion from politics they were supposed to uphold, had come here for prayer sessions. Yet the temple was small and ordinary in a way that was as incongruous with the passions it aroused as it was with the giant *toriis* and the striking path leading to it.

Untroubled by the controversy because of both the unpretentiousness of the location and my belief that the Japanese dead had as much right to be remembered as anyone else, I turned my head to discover that a man in his thirties had knelt down on the stones and begun to pray. His hands were joined together under his chin as though he were a Christian, and his eyes were firmly shut. He wasn't old enough to have lost his father in the war; perhaps he was praying for one of his grandfathers or for all the dead.

On the right, twisted pieces of paper signifying holiness hung on parallel lengths of twine strung between two posts, and next to them was a freestanding sign stating that contributions could be made at the Temple Office. Then, spotting a building a short distance away through whose glass façade the outline of a fighter aircraft was visible, I headed in that direction.

At close quarters I could see a counter inside with a young woman behind it. Her round hat and smart uniform made her look so much like a stewardess that for a second I could have believed I had arrived at an air terminal; but the sign at the door said "Yushukan War Museum". I went in, bought a ticket and began looking at the exhibits.

The explanation in English in front of the aircraft that had caught my eye declared it was a Zero. There were red sun symbols on its wings and either side of the fuselage, but it was painted, not white like the Zeros I was used to seeing in war films, but a dark green that would have made it difficult to spot from enemy aircraft over the jungles of Asia.

Under the field gun in the opposite corner, this time painted brown for camouflage purposes, it was stated it had belonged to the 100th Heavy Artillery Battalion, all of whose members were killed in the "honourable defeat" they suffered during the defence of Okinawa. For some reason, though, no mention was made of the fact that the tiny Okinawa Islands, hundreds of kilometres to the south of the mainland, were the only piece of Japanese territory that the Americans were able to take through ground action, and the fierce resistance they encountered in the process was a major factor in convincing them that they had no option but to resort to the atom bomb.

But the most striking item in this part of the museum was the steam engine standing next to the field gun. Every part of it had been carefully cleaned and polished, and the plate underneath stated that it was the first engine to travel on the Thailand-Burma Railway built during the "Great Southeast Asia War". Apparently it had then been in service on this route for many years before being purchased by veterans of the Railway Brigade and presented to the museum.

Incredulously I read it all again. For the first time I had come across something that genuinely startled me. Just as I had no particular objection to the Japanese dead being remembered, I had no particular objection to Japanese weaponry being displayed either. But the railway mentioned here with such pride was the "Railway of Death" brought into being by using thousands of prisoners of war from Britain, Australia and New Zealand as slave labour. I was reminded of captives with sunken cheeks and prominent ribs toiling under the sun, the ramshackle graves of those dead from dysentery, hunger and the beatings they received, and of the old men, fewer by the year, who congregated outside the Japanese embassy in London from time to time, holding up placards demanding compensation. Perhaps those objecting to Yasukuni had a point.

The room I walked into next seemed to confirm this. As in the Peace Museum in Hiroshima, here, too, large black-and-white photographs accompanied by explanatory comments hung on the walls. The difference was that, while in the Peace Museum Japanese conduct before and during the war was treated with a frankness which had seemed impressive to me (but was perhaps only necessitated by the number of foreign visitors the museum attracted), here, in an atmosphere of "being among friends", even the comments in English were aimed at justifying Japan in every way.

According to the narrative that unfolded on the walls, the United States had first coerced Japan into westernising and then, fearing competition from it, sought to put obstacles in its way. President Roosevelt in particular had been staunchly anti-Japanese throughout the 1930s, and even taken the provocative step of openly supporting Chiang Kai-shek. Unwillingly drawn into war in consequence, Japan had fought bravely in both the Pacific and Southeast Asia, and while it had unfortunately lost, its challenging of Western imperialism had been a source of inspiration to a series of leaders from Ho Chi Minh to Ahmed Suharto in their subsequent liberation struggles. Why ridding Asia of Western imperialism should involve replacing it by Japanese imperialism and why a substantial part of the Asian leaders referred to had been active in resistance movements against the Japanese before taking on the Westerners were not explained.

The last room was devoted to "Those Who Gave Their All for Japan". A kamikaze plane hung from one corner of the ceiling while below was a black *kaiten* torpedo the size of a small submarine, designed to be manually steered to its target before being blown up together with its crew of two. According to the explanation provided, this weapon, adapted from the automatic torpedo developed by the Japanese, which avoided leaving a trail of bubbles behind it by running on oxygen instead of compressed air, had successfully been used against the enemy on many occasions. On the walls were photographs of the 6000 young men and a handful of young women who had gone to their deaths in such suicide weapons.

I walked out of the museum feeling weary, but Yasukuni had one more revelation in store for me. When I got to the outer *torii* of the temple I saw a black van approaching from the left, with the sort of music pouring out of the loudspeakers mounted on its roof that ice cream vans in England use to notify children of their arrival. Mounted across the bonnet, though, was a wire mesh barrier which could only be there as protection against stone-throwing opponents, and when the vehicle parked on the pavement opposite and the music fell silent, two hard-faced young men dressed entirely in black got out and immediately began shouting in unison in a rhythmic way that suggested they were chanting a slogan.

Seeing me staring, "They are *uyokus*," explained a young woman on my side of the road: "nationalist militants. Normally they turn up at weekends when there are more people about. What they are doing here today, I don't know."

"Maybe it's a practice run. What are those words they keep repeating?"

"Respect the Emperor, drive out the barbarian."

"And who is the barbarian?"

She lowered her gaze in embarrassment, "Anyone who isn't Japanese, all foreigners."

"I thought it was forbidden to make hideous noises in these parts."

She was even more embarrassed. "You can be certain that we don't all think like them," she muttered before hurriedly walking away.

I could see how, on a Saturday or Sunday, with the crowd egging the demonstrators on or heckling them, the mood could become more violent, but at the moment, the *uyokus* appeared almost harmless, as if they really were only practicing. Although I was the only barbarian in sight, it was obvious they were not about to take any action to drive me out, and were only interested in spreading their message. After some more time went by without anyone taking an interest in them, they got back in their van and, once again playing their strange ice cream music, drove off.

Coming on top of everything I had seen in the museum, though, the incident had increased my discomfort. As I walked back towards the area surrounding Tokyo Station, I remembered Lafcadio Hearn writing to a Western friend that the Japanese could be "very petty sometimes". But when I reached my destination half an hour later, the executives and young secretaries in thick coats and scarves making up the lunchtime crowds didn't seem to have anything to do with the Yasukuni temple or the war or nationalism. They were neither petty nor grand, just faces passing by. Ceasing to look at them after a while, I stepped into a small restaurant and had my own lunch before setting out for the Ginza.

One of the few works of Lafcadio Hearn I had managed to get hold of and read was a short story about an aged peasant who set fire to the bags of rice that constituted all his worldly goods in order to warn his friends of an imminent tsunami. I had learnt from this tale that tsunamis started with the sea receding to a great distance and all but vanishing from sight, before the process suddenly became reversed and a white line of foam began approaching, rising higher and moving faster all the time. When the first transistor radios had arrived in the West at the end of the 1950s like a white line heralding that the mighty tsunami of the Japanese economy was on its way, they had brought the name "Ginza" with them. It had begun to be used in advertisements for Japanese goods to suggest luxury and quality, and the shopping district to which it belonged had become the one part of Tokyo everyone had heard of.

But Chuo, the broad central avenue of the Ginza a short walk took me to, didn't look particularly luxurious. Despite the packed department stores and pavements, the scarcity of advertising meant there wasn't even an obvious air of consumption. The only detail that made the area a little special was the streetlamps shaped like a squat hexagonal pyramid set atop a taller, inverted one that were more elegant than the ancient streetlamps of Ikebukuro. Like the Eiffel-based Tokyo Tower, they suggested derivation from models in Paris.

The Parisian motif was kept up by the French pastries and the model of the Arc de Triomphe in marzipan in the window of the Tokyo branch of Dalloyau, and by tearooms with names like Dutour and Madeleine. In this respect, the tsunami that had welled up in the 1950s had got stuck in that decade. The Ginza was basically nondescript, but, in part, it was also like a backdrop for a black-and-white film which was set in the Paris of half a century ago.

I spent more than an hour going in and out of department stores like Wako, Mitsukoshi and Matsuzakaya without coming across anything to change these impressions. I then discovered a café on the first floor of another department store that overlooked the corner of Chuo and Harum, and I sat for another half hour at a window-side table, watching the two video hoardings across the way that were the most prominent examples of advertising in the Ginza flicker and change above the traffic and the pedestrians. When I came out, although it was still early, lights were burning in the shops because of the overcast day, and the elegant Parisian streetlamps gleamed like blocks of ice against a sky drained to a murky white by the falling temperature. But it didn't look as if the snow I was expecting would come that day either.

* * *

Tokyo had disappointed me. I knew that the name "Tokyo" given to Edo in the Meiji period when it was decided to make it the country's new seat of government meant "the eastern capital". This had initially been nothing more than a geographical designation, but the eventual transformation of Japan into the richest and most important country in Asia meant that Tokyo now had a broader claim to being the "Capital of the East". I had, without being altogether aware of it, hoped this metropolis would live up to the connotations it evoked, bringing my eastern travels to a climax and summing them up.

But Tokyo didn't even sum itself up. The "mini cities" it consisted of failed to add up to a tangible whole. It wasn't clear what Ikebukuro, behind whose office blocks there were traditional Japanese houses at one end and karaoke bars and pachinko parlours at the other, had in common with the high walls and dying plants of the Emperor's palace, or what linked the surroundings of the Yasukuni temple, where fanatical *uyokus* roamed, to the Ginza's dreams of Paris. Such fragmentation might be encountered in all big cities to some extent, but it seemed to have reached extraordinary dimensions here.

I had decided to use the last day of my stay to visit Shibuya and Shinjuku, said to be the two most typical corners of contemporary Tokyo. But when I finally went out after once again waiting for the morning rush hour to be over, I first took the Yamanote Line to Ueno Park.

The enormous open space I found was located on a hill that suddenly rose in the middle of the mostly flat city. Because this had been the northern edge of Edo, the Tokugawas had had a large temple built here to protect their city from evil and, ironically, it was also at this spot that they had made their desperate last stand against Emperor Meiji's forces in the Battle of Ueno. At the entrance of the park was a shrine dedicated to their fallen warriors.

Despite its historic importance the area was only slightly less neglected than the grounds of the Imperial Palace, and the homeless sleeping here and there under sheets of cardboard on the benches amongst patches of snow indicated that the economic crisis in the Far East was felt in Japan, too. All the same, I managed to wander about for so long, looking at the Tokugawas' old temple, a pagoda a short distance away from it, and an artificial lake in one corner of which a fleet of swan-shaped pedalos awaited the return of summer that by the time another forty-five-minute train ride brought me to Shibuya it was past two o'clock.

It was clear, though, that even if most of those in the city were at work at this time of day, there were plenty of others who didn't have to be. The large main square, rendered the most advertisement-rich spot I had come across in Japan by a profusion of video hoardings, was infinitely more crowded than the Ginza. Everywhere the heads of the throngs flowing along the pavements bobbed up and down, and whenever the lights in the roads opening into the square changed to red, a sight that could perhaps be seen only in Tokyo occurred, with the traffic stopping and the black-and-white stripes at the mouth of each road being revealed for a second before disappearing again under the feet of those crossing to the other side.

Turning my back on the main shopping area to explore the maze of streets off a road climbing up at a steep angle on the left, I came across another sight peculiar to the city. The function of the small hotels that seemed to be everywhere was indicated as much by the reliefs in the shape of women's faces and red hearts that decorated their façades as by the names like *Passion*, *Love House* and *White Satin* that they bore in English. These had to be the "love hotels" where Tokyo couples living in cramped flats hired a room for an hour or two to make love away from their children or parents.

Feeling that my urge to look at the world, which had made me go to see the dead at the vast war cemetery in Singapore, was now forcing me to do something even more questionable, and yet unable to stop myself, I began going in and out of the hotels. But the nearly identical lobbies designed to minimise embarrassment offered barely enough light to see by, and in each case "Reception" was only a booking window where the person serving sat behind a heavily tinted pane of glass that left only their hands visible. Nobody paid any attention to my examining the images, some dark, others lit up, of rooms furnished with naked statues or round beds or ceiling mirrors that were displayed on an electronic panel in one corner for guests to choose from.

By the time I left the third or fourth hotel I had figured out that the images in darkness represented the rooms that were taken. Thinking about my idle mind having added this detail to all the others it had collected, I made my way back to the bottom of the hill, had a late lunch in a busy café and, after walking about some more in Shibuya, boarded my third train of the day and travelled to Shinjuku as it was beginning to get dark.

One of the exits from the station was marked, with a hint of pride, as the "Skyscraper District". Outside, the tallest structures in the city, the Tokyo Metropolitan Government Building and a handful of giant hotels, stood with row upon row of lit windows under the sky which seemed to have turned violet more because of the cold than because of the failing light. The scene was indeed not without a certain grandeur: even the crows making their last flight of the day over their territory seemed to be a little more subdued and respectful than usual.

When I crossed over to the other side of the station I discovered it was even more impressive. The neons on the stores in the area, bigger than even the stores of Shibuya, seemed to say that all their predecessors I had come across had been a mere rehearsal and the real performance was here. Everywhere coloured lights flashed on and off, opened and closed like fans, spun round themselves, filled a rectangular frame by running from one end of it to the other before running back and starting again. At this spot Tokyo was less a real city than a video game that constantly undid and remade itself. But, like the snow that had failed to arrive for days, that sense of a summing up I was after was still absent.

Nonetheless, something striking did eventually occur. Because I had to wait again, this time for the evening rush hour to be over, I arrived at my hotel just after nine o'clock and went to bed immediately to be able to get up in time for my early flight. I then couldn't fall asleep for hours, but I finally drifted off and in a dream I had towards morning I found myself with Lafcadio Hearn.

We were sitting on the floor on either side of a low table in a traditional Japanese house with a silvery light streaming in through the paper-covered windows that suggested it was snowing outside. Hearn was dressed, Japanese style, in a long silk robe with a belt around the waist, and I was wearing a suit I remembered last seeing draped over a chair somewhere, and a broad-brimmed hat I couldn't take off because of the chill in the room.

"I am an Irishman born in Greece," Hearn was saying. "Do you know what it's like to be familiar with Mediterranean culture but not be a part of it?"

"No," I replied.

"How about being familiar with British culture but not being a part of that? Do you know what that's like?"

"No."

"Then I learned French, and when I was nineteen I moved to Ohio. The Midwest is an unbelievable place: those who spend any time on those flat, endless plains under a flat, endless sky come to feel there is no fixed point they can take their bearings from, and they lose all sense of belonging somewhere."

He stopped and looked at me hopefully once again, but, "I've never been in those parts," I told him.

"If we were not so different, you might have understood me," he said sadly. Then he began telling me how people like him lost the ability to form ties, how their hearts became "like the frozen wastes of the North" and they turned into drifters going from place to place, looking at everything through the eyes of a stranger. But this was not all bad, for it was also these people who – because they did not regard the world as their home and take it for granted – could see and describe how peculiar and remarkable it was.

I had taken as much of this as I could stand. I interrupted him to tell him that these were mere excuses, and those who kept going from place to place did so, not because they had a surname derived from a word that meant "to wander", or because they were exposed to vastly different cultures or became fluent in a foreign language as a child, or – and this was the most ludicrous excuse of all – the Midwest had a strange effect on them, but because subconsciously they were afraid of death and its no less frightening twin, failure. Becoming a stranger everywhere was not something that just happened to them, but something they actively cultivated because they felt that if they ever settled anywhere, ever became anything definite, they would start surrendering to the pair they feared; and so, to avoid becoming a stationary target, they kept on the move, kept running away. But, as time went by, they grew old and tired, and the world stopped seeming intoxicatingly full of possibilities and came to seem only strange and frightening. By then, however, going was all they knew, and so they kept going, like wind-up toys that could not refrain from moving. Those were the simple origins and the equally simple end of that great, mystical activity called "travel".

I had no idea whether the things I said were any truer than the things my companion had said, or explained our lives any better. But I was speaking with such conviction that he was taken aback. He rose hastily, saying, "I must go," and, after a second's pause, attaching to my name the syllable the Japanese use to express respect, added, "*Sayonara, Savkar-san.*"

For a moment I savoured the pleasure of having defeated him. But, like every dream, this one, too, had a logic of its own, and the man who actually walked out of the door with the all-revealing cold light of snow visible round its edges was not Hearn but I in my suit and broad-brimmed hat – while I also stood in the middle of the room, watching myself go.

When I opened my eyes at this point I saw that it had finally started to snow in the night. I stopped my alarm clock, still with ten minutes to go before it rang, and went and stood at the window. The roofs of Ikebukuro were white, and small flakes were still coming down from the sky. The intersecting tyre marks left by early cars in the street below looked like Japanese characters from this height. Soon the pavements would be filled with those on their way to work, and the city would embark on a new, wintry day. But all these details had somehow become unimportant to me. I turned away, quickly got dressed, slipped my passport and ticket into my pocket, and, doing the only thing I could, walked out of the door as I had done in my dream.

THE ALTINEL MUSEUM

When I stepped outside, the snow had got heavier, and the pines and the birches across from the Mannerheim Museum were fast losing their shape under a fresh layer of whiteness. I slowly made my way down the hill, gazing at the frozen sea through the gaps between the elaborate wooden Scandinavian houses in the darkness that was already falling.

It was as if, in the split second between my reaching for the doorknob after slipping away from the guided tour of the Field Marshal's former home and my emergence into the street, I had lived through my travels in the Far East once again, starting out in the fierce heat and sunshine of Malaysia and Singapore and going on to the cooler climate of Hong Kong and Macao, followed by the strong winds of Busan and the grey rain of Shanghai, before the snow that finally fell in Tokyo had led me to cold and white Helsinki.

Looking at my wanderings as a single unified journey towards winter in this way, I could also see they had been accompanied by a steady reduction of my burning desire for travel till it had dwindled into a solitary icy blue flame which stubbornly kept going but gave off little warmth or light. Nor was that the full extent of the change I had undergone. I remembered that someone had said the aim of travel should be not to see foreign countries but to reach the stage where we could see our own country as foreign. That, though, was a trick that even the most inexperienced traveller mastered quite early on. A more advanced stage came with our beginning to see ourselves, too, as foreign, a stranger we had somehow fallen in with during our travels and didn't find particularly interesting or likeable. When this happened our lives stopped being our lives and became just a museum we were wandering in.

Helsinki was a city of odd museums (the Museum of Workers' Housing, the Tram Museum). In fact, the whole world was a series of museums of one kind or another, some, like that eccentric Museum of Workers' Housing and its companion dealing with trams, devoted to just the background and décor of our lives, some, like the airless, dusty Museum of History and Ethnography in Malacca, the giant War Museum in Seoul, the bleak Peace Museum in Hiroshima, and the absurd nationalistic Yushukan Museum in Tokyo, to our spectacular collective follies, and some, like the remote and virtually deserted Lafcadio Hearn Museum in Matsue, to our private obsessions and consolations. There was nothing and no one that couldn't be summed up by a collection of exhibits placed in a museum for visitors to view with a degree of detachment and move on. Having realised on a visit to yet another museum that this was all that my recent travels in the Far East or anything else I had ever experienced could reveal to me, it wasn't long before I found myself at the recently opened Altinel Museum.

The two-storey building was in a snowy street on the outskirts of a northern city not unlike Helsinki. The door turned out to be unlocked when I pushed it, but there was no one inside. A notice apologised for the rooms on the ground floor devoted to Altinel's life in Turkey and America still remaining inaccessible to visitors weeks after the official launch of the museum, and promised they would open as soon as the correct arrangement of their contents was decided on. Yet the firmness with which their doors seemed to be shut made it hard not to wonder if they would really be opened ever again.

Hearing my footsteps echo in the empty building, I climbed to the upper storey devoted to Altinel's wanderings, and located the room identified as "Travels in the Far East".

At the entrance were a set of panels with blown-up reproductions of entry and exit stamps from Altinel's passport. Altinel had collected these strange marks in a variety of shapes and colours with the almost perverse fascination that drives others to collect matchboxes or beermats, postcards or autographs, and sometimes studied them for minutes at a time. Now they were there for the visitor to study as well.

Immediately below a rectangular black stamp indicating that on 19 September 1999 the Immigration Affairs Authority had granted Altinel 30 days' leave to enter Singapore "for a social visit" was a circular green stamp indicating he had left the country for Malaysia the next day via the border crossing at Woodlands. To avoid invalidating their claim that the railway station in Singapore belonged to them and using it already constituted entry into their territory, the Malaysians had refrained from giving Altinel an entry stamp, but they had placed a triangular red exit stamp in his passport at Johor Baharu when he returned to Singapore by bus three days later. The entry and exit stamps from Hong Kong in a peculiar shade between navy blue and purple were completely clear while those from Macao were grey and vague like the city itself. Being superimposed, Korea's oval stamps were not particularly legible either. The visa issued by the People's Republic of China took up an entire page, and two bilingual stamps in Japanese and English showed Altinel had passed through Japan in February 2003. This collection of symbols denoting movement and escape seemed like an apt summation of a life spent not doing something requiring patience and effort such as working or raising children but just drifting about the world.

But there were other exhibits as well. The glass cases hanging at regular intervals on the two side walls all the way down the length of the room contained items picked up at hotels by Altinel who, far from sharing the feelings of displacement and unease experienced by many at such establishments, had always felt oddly safe under their roof. A sheet of writing paper decorated with Islamic motifs from the Hotel Istana in Kuala Lumpur, a bar of soap still in its wrapper with the name "Hotel Lisboa" printed on it, a small bottle of aftershave supplied to the guests of the Peace Hotel in Shanghai and a pen from the Hotel Granvia in Hiroshima were some of the items on display. I couldn't help wondering for a moment why someone had found these tawdry souvenirs worth keeping, before I walked over to the horizontal cases placed in a row down the middle of the room.

The first case had English-language newspapers in it from various countries. The period covering Altinel's travels in the East had been marked by the rise and fall of economies, the handover of colonies, the heightening of tensions between enemy states and even the building of new cities. But, less interested in these "Great Events" than in the details of daily life, Altinel had scoured the papers he bought, for local news and small ads, inhaled the smell of foreign paper and ink, and at times wondered if some peculiarity in the English of a sentence he was reading was the result of direct translation from the writer's native tongue. Copies of the *New Straits Times*, the *South China Morning Post*, the *Korea Herald* and the *Daily Yomiuri* that lay in the case were evidence of these obsessions.

The next case held banknotes and coins acquired by Altinel in the countries he visited. I saw ringgit notes bearing the likeness of the Sultan of Malaysia, colourful dollar bills issued by the Hong Kong Special Administrative Region accompanied by coins with a scalloped edge and the head of Queen Elizabeth II that had still been in circulation at the time of Altinel's visit, Korean won with pictures of temples, and Chinese yuan kept crisp and new by an economy where deflation and a general absence of anything worth buying prevented money from changing hands with any frequency. Finally, there came Japanese yen with portraits of politicians dressed in the winged collars and tails of the 1930s.

Of course flags, too, were amongst items that Altinel had noticed and described at some length in his writings, and the third case was occupied by postcard-sized versions of the American-style red-and-white-striped flag to be seen everywhere in Malaysia, the five-starred flag on the dome of the Supreme Court of Singapore, the Hong Kong flag with its bauhinia and the Macao flag with its lotus, the Korean flags on sale outside Tapgol Park in Seoul, the red flag flying on the high rooftops of Shanghai and the Japanese flag Altinel had seen hanging absolutely motionless from its pole in the midst of the snow outside Matsue Castle.

The last of the horizontal cases contained two of the cheap notebooks with a blue cover used by Altinel when travelling, one closed, the other lying open so that the viewer could see the writer's strange, illegible scrawl. Despite his misgivings Altinel had gone on not only travelling but also writing in an effort to put the strangeness he perceived in the world into words, occasionally excitedly believing that the sights he had seen did almost come alive under his hand as it rapidly formed the letters, but more often despairing because what he managed to come up with seemed so inadequate and lifeless to him. Like the stamps on the pages of his passport, though, the marks left by his pen on these pages, too, pointed to a quest which was now alien to me.

It was only as I was lifting my head from looking at the notebooks that I noticed the small globe that was the only object in a vertical case standing against the wall at the bottom of the room. The names of the continents on it were written in Korean, and sailing ships resembling the galleons of the old explorers had been drawn on the oceans. Because it was standing on a glass shelf it looked as if it were suspended in space, and a tiny spotlight in one corner of the case lit up half of it like a miniature sun. Altinel, who describes seeing an identical globe at Nandaemun Market in Seoul in his account of Korea, had been unable to resist buying this one when he spotted it several days later in a shop in Busan that was about to close, and for months afterwards he had remembered the details of the evening he could see outside through the glazed door – the city with the setting sun behind it, green-and-white buses, schoolgirls in uniforms resembling the sailor suits worn by Edwardian children – as he waited for his purchase to be wrapped.

For a moment I looked at the plastic sphere, hardly bigger than a fist, with its inscriptions in the unfamiliar Hangul script, and thought that, contrary to what Altinel believed, the world was actually small and ordinary, and it was only all that was written on it that made it seem otherwise. Then, taking advantage of the fact that no one was about, I did something terrible. Opening the case, I removed the globe, still warm from the spotlight, rotated it on the tips of my fingers to set it spinning and let go. It bounced once, before hitting the floor again and breaking into a few large pieces which almost immediately broke into smaller ones, with these breaking into smaller ones still, so that what Altinel had always feared – but, because, in the strange dynamics of life, the things we fear are often also the very things we yearn for, had perhaps secretly wanted as well – occurred and the oceans, continents, countries and cities and all they contained were enveloped in darkness and disappeared while I, seemingly doomed to look and see until the last moment, went on watching.